"I wish I knew why I make you nervous."

Dale hadn't planned to open that can of worms. But the words had spilled out before he could contain them.

For a second, Christine seemed taken aback by his comment. He thought she was going to deny it, but instead she said, "Look, you seem like a nice man, Sheriff. I'm sorry if I've offended you. It's nothing personal. I just think it's wise if we keep our distance."

"Why?"

"It's a very long story."

"I don't have to be anywhere for an hour."

Her lips tipped into a mirthless smile. "That wouldn't even cover chapter one. Let it go."

Dale knew that no matter what he said next, she wasn't going to budge today. So he murmured a quick goodbye and headed back to his patrol car.

But as he pulled down the drive, he was determined that sooner or later he would uncover the real meaning behind the name of Christine's business, Fresh Start Farm.

Books by Irene Hannon

Love Inspired

IRENE HANNON

An author of more than twenty-five novels, Irene Hannon is a prolific writer whose books have been honored with both the coveted RITA® Award from Romance Writers of America and a Reviewer's Choice Award from *Romantic Times BOOKreviews*.

A former corporate communications executive with a Fortune 500 company, she now devotes herself to writing full-time. Her emotionally gripping books feature hope-filled endings that highlight the tremendous power of love and faith to transform lives.

In her spare time, Irene performs in community musical theater productions and is a church soloist. Cooking, gardening, reading and spending time with family are among her favorite activities. She and her husband make their home in Missouri—a favorite setting for many of her novels!

Irene invites you to visit her Web site at www.irenehannon.com.

Where Love Abides
Irene Hannon

Steeple
Hill®

Published by Steeple Hill Books™

STEEPLE HILL BOOKS

Steeple
Hill®

ISBN-13: 978-0-373-81357-5
ISBN-10:   0-373-81357-0

WHERE LOVE ABIDES

For he has freed my soul from death, my eyes from tears, my feet from stumbling.
—*Psalms* 116:8

To Dr. Andrew Youkilis—
With deepest gratitude for your surgical skill,
compassionate care and
extraordinary kindness

Chapter One

Great. Just great.

Sheriff Dale Lewis regarded the small pickup truck on the shoulder of the road, facing the wrong way and tilted at an odd angle. It looked like his already long day was about to get longer.

Stifling a sigh, he took a final sip of tepid coffee and eased his patrol car off the wet pavement. As he settled the disposable cup back into the holder, he scanned the truck, illuminated in the glare of his headlights. It had Missouri plates and looked brand-new, but he'd never seen it before. Must not belong to anyone around Oak Hill. He knew most of the vehicles from his hometown on sight.

As he keyed the license number into the laptop beside him and waited for the results to appear on the screen, he surveyed the drenched landscape. Considering how dry the entire month of August had been, he knew the area farmers would consider the much-needed rain a blessing.

But he suspected the driver of the truck wouldn't agree. The pavement could be dangerously slick around this bend when dampened after a dry spell, as the person behind the wheel had discovered. It was too dark to see the road, but he figured he'd find skid marks come daylight.

When the license information came back, he gave it a quick scan. The vehicle was registered to a Christine Turner, and everything was clean. The name seemed familiar somehow, but he couldn't place it. And he was too tired to try. If she'd been the driver, she must have called a family member or friend to pick her up and abandoned the car until daylight.

Not that he blamed her. It was pitch-dark, and he was pretty sure the respite from the earlier downpour was temporary. Lightning continued to zigzag through the sky in the distance, and the ominous rumble of thunder suggested the imminent arrival of another deluge.

The truck was far enough off the highway not to cause problems, but the driver should have put the emergency flashers on, he reflected. Hoping the vehicle wasn't locked, he retrieved a flashlight and flipped on the spotlight mounted near his sideview mirror. He needed to check it out anyway, as a matter of routine. He could take care of the flashers at the same time.

He circled the truck first, noting that the engine

was still pinging. Meaning it hadn't been there long. One back tire was fender-deep in mud, but otherwise nothing seemed amiss. Completing his circuit, he checked the driver-side door. Unlocked. Good.

Pulling it open, Dale started to climb up, then froze. The cab wasn't empty. A woman lay sprawled on the seat, one limp arm dangling toward the floor.

A surge of adrenaline shot through him, and Dale squeezed into the cab, balancing one knee on the seat as he leaned over the woman. Pushing aside the shoulder-length light auburn hair that had fallen across her face, he pressed two fingers against her neck. A solid, strong pulse beat a steady rhythm against them, and he let out a slow breath. During his twelve years as a cop in L.A. he'd come upon too many of these kinds of scenes with far different results. The woman might be injured, but at least she was alive.

As Dale set the flashlight down and pulled out his cell phone, he studied her profile. Caucasian, midthirties—and with a very nasty bump on her left temple. He couldn't see any other damage, but her legs were encased in jeans and only a sun-browned length of arm was visible beneath the short sleeves of her cotton shirt. It was possible she'd sustained other injuries that weren't apparent.

Before he could tap in the numbers to summon an ambulance, the woman stirred and gave a slight moan. As he leaned over her again, her eyelids flickered open.

"Ma'am, please don't move. I'm calling an ambulance." Dale kept his voice soft, trying not to startle her.

It didn't work. Jerking her head toward his looming presence, she winced and tried to sit up, but he put out an arm to restrain her.

"Please, ma'am. You've been injured. It would be better if you didn't move until the EMTs check you out."

His soothing tone, meant to calm, seemed to have the opposite effect on her. She stared up at him in the dim light of the cab, blinking as if trying to focus, until all at once fear ignited in her eyes. Fumbling for the door handle on the passenger side, she twisted it open and pushed, scrambling away from him and sliding to the ground with such speed and agility that his mouth dropped open.

Then she slammed the door in his face.

It took a second for his brain to kick back into gear, and by the time he recovered enough to back out of the cab and circle the truck, she was clutching a length of board she must have retrieved from the back, holding it like a baseball bat.

Slowing his approach, Dale assessed the situation. It was obvious the woman was injured. She was using the body of the truck for support and seemed to be having trouble focusing. It was also clear that she was frightened. He had no idea why, but he needed to calm her down.

"Ma'am, you don't need to be afraid. I'm a police officer."

"I can see that." Her voice wasn't quite steady, but her grip on the piece of wood was firm. He had no doubt she'd take a swing at him if he got too close. Had she been drinking? he wondered. But he'd smelled no alcohol, nor seen any evidence of it, in the cab of her truck. Perhaps the bump on her head had muddled her brain. He tried again.

"Look, you need help. I was getting ready to call an ambulance when you came to. Why don't you sit in the truck and take it easy until you get some medical attention? I'll help you."

He took a step toward her, and she raised the board. "I don't need help. Just back off."

Pausing, Dale regarded her through narrowed eyes. Her reaction to his presence was weird. And suspicious, considering he was a uniformed police officer. A warning light began to flash in his brain.

"You're hurt, and your truck isn't going anywhere tonight." He spoke in a slow, deliberate manner. "If you don't want medical assistance, which I strongly recommend, is there someone I can call who could pick you up?"

"No."

"Can I give you a lift home?"

"No. I—it's not far. I can walk."

"Ma'am, it's pitch-dark, and you're in no condition to walk anywhere." She was beginning to waver a bit, and it seemed to take every bit of her concentration to maintain focus. "Be reasonable."

Instead of responding, she edged toward the back of the truck, continuing to lean against it for support. Dale remained where he was, fists on his hips, brow furrowed. In all his years as a cop, he'd never met with a reaction quite like this. While he'd had accident victims refuse medical attention, he'd never encountered such fear and hostility in a comparable situation. It seeped through her pores, almost tangible in its intensity.

When she got to the rear bumper, she pushed off and began to back away from him into the darkness. It was starting to rain again, large drops that left big, dark splotches on the blue cotton of her shirt. In another couple of minutes, they'd both be soaked. Whether she liked it or not, he couldn't let her walk away.

He took two steps in her direction, watching as terror gripped her features. She raised the piece of wood, but suddenly lost her grip on it and swayed. Dale closed the distance between them in three long strides, just in time to catch her before she went facedown in the mud, looping one arm under her knees. Despite her half-conscious state, she fought him, struggling to escape from his grip, every muscle in her lean body tense.

"Please, ma'am. Try to relax. I'm not going to hurt you. But you need medical attention. If you don't want me to call an ambulance, I'll contact our doctor in Oak Hill. I'm sure he'll meet us at his office."

The rain intensified, and without giving her a chance to respond, he headed toward the patrol car, depositing her in the passenger seat. Leaning close, he stared into her dull, slightly glazed dark brown eyes. "Stay put. I don't want to have to go chasing after you in this rain. Nor do I want to have to charge you with interfering with the duties of a police officer." He closed the door, praying the threat he'd pulled out of thin air would work.

It must have, because she was still sitting there after he retrieved her purse from the floor of the truck, locked the doors of her vehicle and slid into his seat in the patrol car. Either that, or she was too hurt to offer further resistance.

Handing over her purse, he pulled out his phone and punched in a number, watching her while it rang.

"Sam? Dale. Listen, sorry to have to ask this, but could you meet me at your office? I've got a woman who's been injured in a car accident and she doesn't want me to call an ambulance. She was unconscious when I found her, and she has a nasty bump on her temple." Dale listened for a few moments, answered a couple of questions, then severed the connection.

As he reached forward to turn the key in the ignition, the woman shrank back as far as possible into the corner of the front seat. She didn't look at him once during the ten-minute drive. Nor did she speak. And the instant the car came to a stop in front of the medical office, she groped for her door handle.

"I control the locks," he told her. "I'll help you out."

As Dale circled the car, he noted Sam's vehicle parked in front of the building. The town physician must have left as soon as he'd received the call, which didn't surprise Dale. After two years in Oak Hill, Sam Martin had become a valued member of the community, and his responsiveness was already legendary.

Once Dale reached her door, he released the locks and pulled it open. She was clutching her shoulder purse against her chest, her expression wary, and she ignored the hand he extended, struggling to stand on her own. He dropped his hand and kept his distance, but stayed close enough to save her from a fall if she started to nosedive again.

"The office is there." He nodded over his shoulder. A light over the front door illuminated a sign that said Sam Martin, M.D.

Edging around Dale, the woman headed toward the door. Close on her heels, he leaned around her and twisted the knob, pushed the door open, then entered behind her.

A tall, trim man with sandy hair that was brushed with glints of silver at the temples stepped through an inner door. "Hi, Dale."

"Sam. Thanks for coming. I haven't confirmed it yet, but I think your patient's name is Christine Turner." At the woman's startled look, Dale glanced at her. "I ran a license check. Standard procedure. And I'm Dale Lewis, just to make things even. This is Dr. Martin."

"We can worry about the introductions later. Right now that bump needs attention." Sam moved forward and tilted her chin up, scrutinizing the injury.

Interesting, Dale noted. She didn't seem frightened of Sam.

"Any idea how long you were unconscious?" Sam asked her.

"No. I remember sliding across the road, and the truck spun around. I hit my head on the door window. After the truck stopped, I unbuckled my seat belt and leaned down to pick up my purse from the floor on the passenger side. That's the last thing I remember until I saw him—" she gave a short jerk of her head in Dale's direction "—leaning over me."

"I don't think she was out long," Dale offered. "The engine was still pinging when I arrived. A few minutes, tops."

"That's good. So is the fact that your memory of the event is clear. But let's take a look." He stepped aside to usher her into his office, directing his next comment to Dale. "I assume you're going to wait?"

"Yes."

While Sam and Christine disappeared into the examining room, Dale settled into a chair in the waiting area and pulled out his cell phone. Using speed dial, the connection took mere seconds.

"Hi, Mom. Sorry, but I've been delayed again. I came across an accident and had to bring the victim into town. Sam's looking her over now. Everything okay with Jenna?"

He listened for a couple of minutes, a smile tugging at the corners of his mouth, while his mother described the youngster's latest antics. His daughter was a source of joy to both of them, and he was glad once again that he'd come home after Linda died. It was far safer being sheriff of Oak Hill than a street cop in L.A. And he didn't want his daughter to grow up without either parent.

Besides, with his mother willing to watch Jenna most days, he didn't have to resort to day care very often. Both he and Linda had agreed that the decision to have children brought with it a responsibility to raise them. They hadn't believed in delegating that task to an outside service, unless there was simply no other option. He was glad he'd been able to follow through on that commitment.

"Look, I should be wrapping up here in the next half hour," Dale responded when his mother finished the tale of Jenna's latest adventure. "Don't hold dinner any longer. I'll eat later. See you soon."

By the time Dale checked his voice mail at work and returned a couple of calls, Sam appeared in the door to the waiting room, closing it with a soft click behind him. Dale rose and tucked the phone back into its holder.

"Is she okay?"

"I think so. Looks like a mild concussion. I'd feel

better if she had an X-ray, but she's not too receptive to that idea. I've alerted her to the things to watch for and advised her to call me if she experiences any troublesome symptoms. In any case, she needs to take it easy for the next couple of days, and I'd prefer that she not spend tonight alone. It would be better if someone was close by in case she needs help."

"I asked about family. Didn't sound like she had any."

"That's what she said. You were right about her identity, too. She bought the Harrison place a couple of months ago and started an organic farm. Cara's been meaning to call her about supplying the restaurant. My wife always has her ear to the ground for natural ingredients."

Now the pieces fell into place. Dale recalled hearing some talk about the new organic farm a few miles from town. No one had seen much of the owner, but rumor had it that she lived—and worked—alone.

"Maybe I'll run her over to Marge's. The B and B isn't usually that busy midweek."

Sam flashed him a smile. "I like that idea. She'll be well taken care of there."

"Yeah. Marge is a good woman." An answering smile softened Dale's serious demeanor for a brief moment. "Let me ask you something, Sam. Did your patient act a bit… odd…with you?"

Puzzled, Sam regarded the sheriff. "I'm not sure what you mean. She's a little woozy from the bump on her head, but I didn't pick up anything abnormal in her behavior. Why?"

Raking his fingers through his hair, Dale shrugged. "She seemed pretty scared when I tried to help her. And she didn't want me to get anywhere near her. I wondered if alcohol could be causing that reaction, but I didn't detect any evidence of it. Any chance she might be on something else that could produce irrational behavior?"

"I didn't see any indication of that. She was very coherent, and I didn't notice any anxiety while I examined her. Under the circumstances, the behavior I observed seemed normal."

"Okay. Thanks. I'll run her over to Marge's. Sorry again about interrupting your evening. Give Cara my apologies, too."

Grinning, Sam stuck his hands in his pockets. "She's used to far worse, trust me. Compared to my old hours in Philadelphia, Oak Hill is a cakewalk."

The inner door opened, and Christine appeared on the threshold. There was a bit more color in her cheeks, and she was holding an ice pack gingerly against her temple.

"The sheriff has suggested you spend the night at the Oak Hill Inn, Ms. Turner, and I second that motion," Sam told her. "I'd rather you not be alone for the next few hours in case you have any problems."

Expecting an argument, Dale was prepared to

press Sam's point. But to his surprise, the woman capitulated.

"Okay. That might be best."

"Don't hesitate to call me—at any hour—if you need my assistance," Sam added.

"I will. Thank you, doctor."

"I'll drop you off at the inn on my way home." Dale held open the door.

Panic—chased by a hint of revulsion—whipped across her face, and Dale shot Sam a quick "see-what-I-mean?" look. The doctor quirked an eyebrow in acknowledgment. It seemed there was something about Dale in particular that disturbed Christine. But why? He was sure they'd never met.

It didn't matter, of course. Considering she'd already been in town two months and their paths had never crossed, it was unlikely he'd see much of her in the future, either. But for some reason her aversion irked him. It wasn't as if he'd done anything to earn it.

She continued to stand by the door to the inner offices, and Dale sent her a disgruntled look. "I'm already late getting off duty, and I've got a five-year-old waiting to be picked up. So if you're ready…"

Looking from one to the other, Sam stepped in. "I'd be happy to save you a trip, Dale. I've got to stop at the hardware store. I can drop off Ms. Turner, if that's okay with her."

The tightness in her features eased. "Thank you. I'd appreciate it."

Feeling dismissed, Dale folded his arms across his chest. "I'll call the garage and make sure your truck is pulled out of the mud. And I'll run you out there in the morning to get it, if you're up to driving."

He waited, wondering if she'd rebuff that offer, too. But she clamped her lips shut and ignored him, speaking to Sam instead. "I'm ready whenever you are."

"I'll lock up and be right with you."

Without another word, Dale turned on his heel and exited. She hadn't even thanked him for his assistance, he reflected as he strode toward his car. That was downright rude. As for her hostile nervousness in his presence—no way would he classify that as normal behavior.

No matter what Sam said.

Chapter Two

A faint knocking penetrated Christine's slumber, pulling her back to consciousness. There must be someone at the door. Or maybe the pounding was only in her head, which was throbbing just as it used to when…

Her eyes flew open as the painful memories crashed over her, and she sat bolt upright.

Bad mistake.

At the abrupt movement, the hammering in her temples increased and she grabbed her head with both hands. An ice pack beside the pillow registered in her peripheral vision, and more recent memories displaced the older ones. She'd had a car accident. The sheriff had picked her up. She'd spent the night at the Oak Hill Inn.

"Christine?"

A woman's voice came through the door, and Christine gingerly scooted to the edge of the bed and swung her legs to the floor. She recognized the jeans and shirt draped over a nearby chair, but had no idea where she'd gotten the oversized caftanlike nightgown in psychedelic shades of purple and hot pink. She had a vague recollection of slipping it over her head last night, but she'd turned the lamp off because the bright light bothered her. Otherwise she surely would have noticed the loud colors, which did nothing to ease the ache in her temples.

"Christine? Are you awake?" The voice was more anxious this time.

"Yes. Just a moment."

Grasping the post on the elaborate Victorian headboard, she stood. Her legs felt a bit unsteady, but strong enough to support a trip to the door. Moving with caution, she worked her way across the ornate room, which looked as if it had been transported intact from the 1880s. She'd driven by the pale pink, gingerbread-bedecked B and B a few times since moving to Oak Hill from Nebraska, but she'd never been inside until now.

When she pulled open the door, Marge Sullivan, the owner of the inn, was standing on the other side. The woman's attire of orange capri pants and a fluorescent yellow-and-pink tunic top edged with beads tipped Christine off to the source of her borrowed nightclothes. Considering they'd met only once, when Marge had stopped by the farm with a welcome gift of the B and B's signature homemade cinnamon rolls, the older woman's kindness was heartwarming. Even if her taste was a bit on the flamboyant side.

"How are you feeling, dear?" Marge asked.

"Improving, thanks."

"Your color is better. That's a good sign." Marge gave her a swift perusal, her head cocked to one side, and nodded in approval before turning apologetic. "I'm sorry to wake you, but Dale stopped by to drive you to your truck. I told him you were still sleeping, so he said he'd come back in an hour. That was thirty minutes ago."

With a frown, Christine checked her watch. Nine-fifteen. She'd slept for almost twelve hours!

"I had no idea it was this late. I'll get dressed and be down in a few minutes."

"I have some breakfast waiting for you."

Food was the last thing Christine wanted. The pounding in her head had subsided to a dull throb since she'd stopped moving, but her appetite was nonexistent. Nevertheless, she managed a weak smile. "Thanks."

Ten minutes later, after dressing and running a comb through her hair, Christine started down the grand staircase that led to the foyer of the inn, gripping the rail as she took the steps one at a time. She was halfway down when the doorbell rang, and Marge bustled out from the rear of the house to answer it.

Seeing Christine on the steps, the innkeeper called up to her as she passed, "Be careful, dear. Like everything else in this monstrosity of a house, those stairs are overdone. Extra wide. I've almost taken a tumble myself a time or two."

As Marge pulled open the front door, Christine resumed her descent, now more careful and focused than ever. She paid no attention to the rumble of voices until she heard footsteps on the stairs and looked up to find the sheriff taking them two at a time.

On instinct, she tried to back up. But her heel connected with the step behind her and she lost her balance. The sheriff skipped the final two steps and lunged for her as she wavered, his grip firm on her upper arms until she got her footing.

Even then, he didn't release her at once. His steel-blue eyes probed hers, and a muscle twitched in his jaw as he inspected the discolored lump protruding from her temple. In daylight, and at this close range, she could see the fine lines at the corners of his eyes, and a few sprinkles of silver glinted in his dark hair. There was strength in his face, and character, she reflected. The kind that you expected to find in an officer of the law. But she'd been fooled before. And she wasn't about to repeat that mistake.

When she attempted to pull out of his grip, he shifted his attention away from the knot on her forehead, his gaze locking on hers.

"I doubt either of us wants to visit Dr. Martin again." His voice was calm and quiet, but there was an edge to it that hadn't been there last night. "I'm not sure what it is about me you don't like, but I suggest you take my arm going down the steps so we can avoid any more accidents. Considering the size of that lump, I suspect your head is throbbing, and you're probably not as steady as you'd like to be."

For a second, Christine thought about contradicting him. But why argue with the truth? She *would* feel more secure with a solid body beside her—even if it belonged to a cop.

In silence, she slipped her arm in his, aware of the muscles bunching beneath her fingers and of the discrepancy in their heights. She figured he had a good seven or eight inches on her five-foot-five-inch frame. An intimidating size advantage. After reaching level ground, she broke contact at once and edged away.

"You're early, Dale," Marge pointed out. "Christine hasn't had breakfast yet."

"That's okay. I'm not that hungry," Christine assured her.

"Nonsense. You have to eat something. Dale, how about a cup of coffee and one of my famous cinnamon rolls?"

A grin tugged at his mouth, softening the tension that had hardened his jaw when he'd spoken to her, Christine noted. "I could be tempted."

"That's what I figured." Marge tilted her head, her spiky white hair reflecting the rainbow of color streaming through the art glass on the stairwell. "Cara's in the back, but she's getting ready to leave."

Without waiting for a reply, she led the way down a hall and into a kitchen that was as sleek and modern as the rest of the house was classic Victorian. Stainless steel appliances and work surfaces dotted the large room, and a red-haired woman looked up with a smile as they entered.

"Cara, this is Christine Turner. Christine, Cara Martin, chef extraordinaire. She serves gourmet dinners at the inn three nights a week. You met her husband last night, Sam Martin."

The woman moved forward and extended her hand. "Hello, Christine. Welcome to Oak Hill. I'm sorry about your accident."

"Thanks. It could have been worse." Christine returned her handshake and smile.

"Marge has been telling me about your farm. I'd like to talk with you about supplying some ingredients for the restaurant," Cara continued. "We try to feature fresh local products and I'd love to patronize an Oak Hill business."

"I've only been at it two months, so I'm just starting to reap results. But I've got a good supply of herbs and flowers, and I've put in blackberries, raspberries and strawberries. They aren't producing much this year, but I expect by next year I'll have a good crop."

"Where are you selling?"

"The farmers' markets in Rolla and St. James."

"I'm surprised I haven't seen you," Cara observed. "I do some of my shopping there."

"Enough business for today," Marge interrupted. "Christine needs to eat."

"And I bet Dale is going to mooch a cinnamon roll or two." Cara sent him a teasing look.

"I'm not mooching," he protested. "Marge offered."

"Only because you showed up early," the B and B owner retorted. Softening her remark with a smile, she tucked her arm in his and led him to one side of the kitchen, where a small walk-out bay window had been transformed into a cozy dining nook complete with an oak table and chairs. "Have a seat. You, too, Christine."

Dale remained standing as Christine approached, taking his seat only after she chose the one on the opposite side of the table.

"Nice to meet you, Christine. I'll be in touch." Cara slung her purse over her shoulder and wiggled her fingers at Dale as she headed for the back door. "See you around, Sheriff."

The plate that Marge set in front of Christine a few moments later was enough food to feed a sumo wrestler. A *hungry* sumo wrestler, Christine decided, as she inspected the intimidating breakfast. The huge omelet, bursting with cheese, mushrooms and ham, was accompanied by a generous serving of pan-fried potatoes laced with onions, plus a fresh fruit garnish. On her best days, Christine didn't eat much more than an English muffin or a single scrambled egg. And today was definitely not one of her best days.

She looked up to find the sheriff watching her across the table with those discerning—and disturbing—blue eyes that didn't seem to miss a thing. He took a measured sip of his coffee as Marge set a large cinnamon roll in front of him.

"There now. Eat up, both of you." The phone rang, and Marge gave them an apologetic look. "Sorry. Dig in. I'll be back in a couple of minutes. Don't want to lose a customer!"

She hustled down the hall, leaving a heavy silence in her wake. The ticking of the clock on the wall seemed magnified as Christine picked up her fork and surveyed the overflowing plate in front of her, trying to formulate a plan of attack.

"Marge's breakfasts are generous."

At the sheriff's comment, Christine looked his way, then dropped her gaze again to the food. "More than."

"She won't be offended if you take some home."

Once again, she was struck by the man's insight. And by his civility. Despite her "keep your distance" cues and her rudeness—she hadn't even thanked him for coming to her rescue last night, after all—he'd shown up today to drive her back to her truck. She doubted that was one of the local sheriff's required duties. Perhaps he was just being kind. But she was more inclined to believe there was some hidden agenda or ulterior motive. There usually was, based on her experience with small-town cops.

His assessing perusal was disconcerting, so Christine tried to focus on her food. By the time Marge returned, she'd managed to put a slight dent in the omelet. The sheriff, on the other hand, had demolished the cinnamon roll. A few miniscule crumbs were the only evidence it had ever existed.

"Well, you certainly made short work of that." Marge propped her hands on her ample hips as she sized up Dale's plate.

"What else can a man do when faced with the world's best cinnamon roll?" He grinned and took a sip of his coffee.

"Hmph. I think you picked up a knack for that glib Hollywood flattery while you were in L.A." The flush of pleasure that suffused Marge's face, however, belied her chiding comment. "As for you, young lady…" She inspected Christine's plate. "I suspect you're still feeling a bit under the weather."

"I'm not much of a breakfast eater." Christine avoided giving the woman a direct response. "May I take it home? This will be enough for me for the next day or two."

"No wonder you're so thin. I should follow your example. But I like food too much." Marge gave a hearty chuckle and lifted Christine's plate. "I'll wrap this up for you."

While the older woman busied herself at the counter, Dale leaned back in his chair and regarded Christine. "I talked to Al at the garage. He pulled your truck out of the mud first thing this morning.

From what he could see, there didn't appear to be any damage."

"Thank you."

The words sounded forced, and Dale sent her a quizzical look, trying to get a handle on her attitude. She'd been fine with Sam, related well to Marge and Cara. He was the problem, it seemed.

But he suspected there was more to it than that, considering the woman had been in town two months and few people had caught more than a glimpse of her. Although he'd asked his mother a few discreet questions when he'd picked up Jenna last night, she hadn't known much about the organic farmer, either. The reserved Christine Turner was an enigma to the friendly folks of Oak Hill.

What had produced that wariness in her soft brown eyes? Dale wondered as he studied her. What had made her guarded and cautious, unwilling to mingle with the residents of her adopted town? And why was his presence a source of tension and nervousness?

Dale suspected she'd been hurt at some point in her life. He'd seen that look of distrust, anxiety and uncertainty on a woman's face before. His own wife's, in fact, on occasion. Though he'd opened his heart to her, his love hadn't been enough to overcome the problems in her past. To mitigate her cynicism and convince her that he could be a source of emotional support. To banish the demon of depression that had plagued her. Perhaps this woman, too, had suffered a similar trauma.

If she had, he felt sorry for her.

But he also knew there was nothing he could do to help her, just as he'd been unable to help Linda.

Not that she wanted him to, of course. Christine Turner had already posted a large Keep Away sign. And he intended to honor it.

Because the last thing he needed in his life was another woman with problems.

Christine finished the note to Marge and pulled out her checkbook. When she'd prepared to leave the B and B a few days ago, Marge had refused to let her pay for the room. While Christine hadn't wanted to make an issue of it in front of the sheriff, she didn't intend to take advantage of the woman's kindness and hospitality. She could afford a night's lodging. And she didn't want to incur any obligations, to owe anyone anything that could be used to manipulate her. Not that she suspected the affable Marge of such intent. But she hadn't suspected it of Jack, either.

Gazing out the window of her small, two-story farmhouse, Christine suppressed the shudder that ran through her as she thought of the man who'd wooed and won her in a whirlwind courtship that had ful-filled every romantic fantasy she'd ever had. Elegant dinners, dozens of roses, winging to black-tie events on the company plane he'd often piloted. She'd felt like Cinderella.

But her fairy tale had worked in reverse. First had

come the happily-ever-after part, then the bad stuff. Her world had crumbled as she'd realized that Jack's interest and attentions had been a sham, a carefully crafted plan to win a woman who would meet his father's approval and pave the way to the top spot in the family-owned business.

Sudden tears stung her eyes, and she swiped at them in anger. She'd done enough crying, and enough regretting, to last a lifetime. The past was behind her, and tomorrow would be better. Fresh Start Farm was up and running, and while she'd never get rich on her small-scale operation, it allowed her to spend her days in a wholesome environment, in fresh air and open spaces. The income from the farm, combined with the modest returns on the investments she'd made with her smaller-than-expected inheritance from Jack, would allow her to live a comfortable, independent life. One in which she didn't owe anyone a thing. Including Marge.

Pulling her attention back to the present, Christine wrote out the check and signed her name. Her maiden name. That was still an adjustment, after using Barlow for four-and-a-half years. But a good one.

After tucking the check into her note, Christine sealed the envelope and affixed a stamp. That was one obligation out of the way.

As for the sheriff—he'd gone above and beyond in his assistance, and she didn't want to owe him any favors, either. Writing a check wasn't an option, but she recalled his mentioning a young daughter. Maybe she could send the child a gift to repay the debt. A picture book, perhaps. She could order an appropriate one on the Internet and have it shipped to the sheriff's office.

Satisfied with the plan, Christine pulled on a wide-brimmed hat and headed outside. For the first few days after the accident she hadn't felt well enough to work in her garden. Now she had to make up for lost time. But as she stepped into the warm sunlight and drew a deep breath of the pungent, spicy air wafting from the rows of neatly planted herbs, she didn't mind in the least.

There was nowhere else she'd rather be. Here, she was safe. And free.

Chapter Three

"Package came for you while you were out, Dale. I put it on your desk."

The sheriff looked over at his deputy as he closed the office door against the lingering summer heat of early September. "Thanks, Marv. And thanks for covering for me."

"No problem." The deputy stood and stretched. "You sure you don't need me to stay a while longer? Alice is finally putting her foot down about that rose arbor I said I'd replace after we moved here last year, and she'll be waiting for me with saw in hand when I get home. But it's too hot for a garden project."

A grin tugged at the corners of Dale's lips. "Sorry. Can't help you out. You should have thought of that before you took early retirement from that cushy corporate security job and decided to move to the country and live a life of leisure."

The other man snorted. "Leisure my foot! Alice

has a list a mile long. Let me tell you, this deputy gig is a godsend. Gets me out of the house a few times a week at least."

Chuckling, Dale regarded the older man. Except for his bristly gray hair, Marv Wallace didn't look anywhere near his fifty-six years. Fit and tanned, he exuded energy and enthusiasm. And as far as Dale was concerned, Marv was the godsend. The flexibility and availability of the affable, hard-working deputy was a much-appreciated blessing for a single-father sheriff.

Thank goodness the city council had finally seen the logic in having a part-time deputy on call. Oak Hill might be small, but the town did need backup. Marv had been on staff only a few months, but he'd already proven invaluable on a number of occasions.

"Anything going on?" Dale moved to the coffee-maker in one corner and lifted the pot to pour himself a cup of the strong brew.

"Just one call. From a Christine Turner."

Dale swung toward the deputy, pot in hand. "What's the problem?"

"She was out working in her garden early this morning, and a car came by at a high rate of speed, swerved off the road as it came around the bend in front of her place and cut a swath through her pumpkin patch. I took a spin out there, and it's torn up pretty good. She got a license number, though."

If she'd been close enough to see the license, she'd been close enough to get hit, Dale realized. His mouth settled into a grim line and he set down the coffeepot. "Did you run it?"

"Yep. Registered to Les Mueller."

"Sounds like Stephen is at it again." Les owned one of the state's biggest dairies and was the largest employer for miles around. But he'd been having problems with his seventeen-year-old son.

"That's what I figured. She said there were three teenage males in the car."

Fisting his hands on his hips, Dale shook his head. "I don't know what's going on with that kid. This is the third time in the past six months he's been involved in some sort of minor incident with the law. Except this time, it could have been a lot worse. Chri...Ms. Turner could have been hit."

"I pointed that out to her."

"Where's the complaint?"

"She didn't file one."

Dale frowned. "She called to report the incident, we made a positive I.D., and she doesn't want to press charges?"

"Nope." Marv sat on the edge of his desk and folded his arms across his chest. "You ever meet her?"

"Yeah. A couple of weeks ago. Her truck skidded off the road the night we had all that rain. I found her unconscious behind the wheel as I was driving by. Brought her in to see Sam. Why?"

The deputy arched his eyebrows. "You never mentioned that."

"Nothing much to mention." Dale reached again for the coffeepot, using that as an excuse to look away. He wasn't sure why he hadn't told Marv about the incident. But something about it had left him unsettled, and he hadn't been inclined to dwell on the encounter.

"Hmph." From Marv's speculative tone, it was clear that Dale's response didn't satisfy him. But the deputy let it pass. "Anyway, did you pick up any odd vibes from her?"

Dale shot him a probing look as he finished pouring his coffee. "What do you mean, odd?"

"I can't quite put my finger on it. She just seemed nervous around me, and she kept her distance. I never invaded her personal space, but whenever I got within a few feet of her, she backed up. I wondered if it was me, or if she's like that with everybody."

Interesting, Dale reflected. "She was that way with me, too. But she seemed fine around Sam and Marge."

"Must be the uniform. You run any stats on her?"

"No reason to. The plates came back clean, and she didn't break any laws."

"Curious thing, though."

"At the moment, I'm more curious about why she didn't want to press charges."

"Can't give you an answer to that, either. I ran the license while I was there, and told her who the car belonged to. She asked me a few questions about Les, and after I explained who he was, she got this real cold look and said to forget it. I told her Les would make things right, but she didn't want to pursue it."

"Stephen needs to be called to task for this. Reckless driving is a serious matter. And if he'd hit Ms. Turner, he could be facing involuntary manslaughter charges."

"The lady didn't seem convinced that anything good would come of pursuing this."

"Okay. Let me think about this one." Frustrated, Dale raked his fingers through his hair. "In the meantime, Alice is waiting for you."

The man rolled his eyes. "I think I'll stop by Gus's first and grab some lunch."

"Boy, you must be desperate!" Grinning, Dale took a sip of his coffee. "With your fitness regime I can't believe you're willing to ingest all that fat to delay the inevitable." Gus's fried food was legendary. Dale figured the diner owner operated on a simple philosophy: if it could be breaded, it could be fried.

"I'll do almost anything to avoid a date with that saw. See you around."

As the man disappeared through the front door, Dale strolled toward his office. After twelve years in a cramped, cookie-cutter cube in L.A., illuminated only by harsh fluorescent light, he never failed to appreciate his sunny Oak Hill office, with all its homey touches—including multiple pictures of Jenna displayed on the oak bookshelves that occupied most of one wall.

He took a few seconds to enjoy them, as he always did after settling in behind his desk, starting with a photo of her the day she was born, her pink face scrunched into a howl. From there he moved on to each year's birthday picture, a smile tugging at his lips as he perused them, enjoying her progress from infant to toddler to a little girl with long blond hair and merry blue eyes. What a blessing she'd been in his life.

And her birth had provided an unexpected blessing in his often-difficult marriage as well, he recalled. As he and Linda had lavished their love on their daughter, they'd grown closer. Linda had come to appreciate—and believe in—the depth of Dale's caring, and he had been touched by the fierce protectiveness she'd displayed toward Jenna.

The tiny baby had breached the walls around her heart far more effectively than he ever had, Dale reflected, giving him a glimpse of the woman his wife could have been under different circumstances. In fact, the last few months of his wife's life had been the happiest time in their marriage.

A wave of sadness lapped at the edges of his consciousness, and Dale forced himself to move on to the next photo, from Jenna's fifth birthday early in the summer. Her sunny smile helped dispel his melancholy, and he turned his attention to the package Marv had placed on his desk.

It was a large, flat envelope with a return address he didn't recognize. Slitting the end, he slid the contents onto his desk. A colorful children's book emerged, along with a packing slip.

Puzzled, Dale looked inside the envelope, but found nothing else. He picked up the book, an oversized volume with colorful, imaginative illustrations titled, *The Reluctant Princess*. The medallion on the cover indicated it had won a prestigious children's book award. Jenna would love it. But who had sent it?

Picking up the packing slip, he found his answer.

Thanks for your assistance the night of the accident. I hope your daughter enjoys this.
Christine Turner.

Taken aback by her unexpected thoughtfulness, Dale examined the gift. She might not want anything to do with him—or Marv either, based on the man's account of his experience today—but apparently she hadn't been as ungrateful as she'd seemed the night he'd come to her assistance.

And now he felt guilty. Although he hadn't been happy about Christine's refusal to file a complaint, he'd told himself it was her business and had planned to write it off. If it had been anyone else, however, he'd have paid a call and pushed the victim to take the next step. His well-honed sense of right and wrong had always prodded Dale to go the extra step, to put himself on the line if necessary to ensure that justice was done.

Not that he always succeeded. Almost a dozen years as an L.A. street cop had taught him that life wasn't always fair. And those lessons had been reinforced as he'd watched the woman he loved struggle with the lingering, destructive effects of betrayal and abuse.

Without his faith, he would have become a cynic years ago. But prayer sustained him. And he need look no further than the Bible to find plenty of examples of unfairness. Jesus Himself had been treated unjustly.

Yet Dale wasn't passive about injustice. As far as he was concerned, wrongs that could be righted should be. That was one of the reasons he'd become a cop. To put authority on the side of those who might feel powerless. To help redress wrongs.

And Christine Turner had been wronged.

Whatever her reasons for refusing to press charges, Dale couldn't let it rest without attempting to convince her to reconsider. Stephen Mueller wasn't a bad kid, but he needed to be taught a lesson or these minor incidents could evolve into far more serious offenses. A formal complaint from Christine might be the wake-up call he needed. Besides, Dale owed it to the town to follow up on this before Stephen caused a serious problem. Even if it was uncomfortable.

Grabbing his cup of coffee, Dale strode toward the door, convinced he was doing the right thing. But he also knew that a certain organic farmer wasn't going to be thrilled to see him.

Disheartened, Christine leaned on her shovel and surveyed the remains of her pumpkin patch. She'd been working steadily since those wild teenagers had skidded through the garden early that morning, but the damage was extensive. As she'd filled in the ruts and salvaged as many vines as possible, her dreams of an autumn pumpkin patch, complete with apple cider and cookies, had begun to evaporate. She estimated that at least half her crop had been destroyed.

Wiping her forehead with the back of her hand, she resettled her wide-brimmed hat on her head, hoisted the shovel again and went back to work. There was little traffic on this byway during the week, but she'd done her research and knew that come fall, the colorful Missouri foliage would draw leaf-watchers from as far away as St. Louis. That's why she'd planted her pumpkin patch close to the road. Adorned with a colorful scarecrow and welcoming signs, she'd hoped to attract passersby. Now she wasn't sure she'd be able to salvage enough to follow through with her plan.

The hum of an approaching car caught her attention, but she didn't spare it a glance—until she heard the vehicle slow and turn into her driveway.

When she looked up and saw the police car, her heart skidded to a stop and the breath jammed in her throat. It was a familiar reaction, one she'd experienced every time she'd had any contact with the world of law enforcement over the past few years. Trying to rein in her panic, she watched as the sheriff emerged from the car. He assessed the damage, fists on his hips, before striding toward her.

"Good afternoon, Ms. Turner."

"Sheriff." Her voice was stiff and tight.

His tone, on the other hand, was conversational. "I heard there was a problem out here this morning."

"I've already discussed it with your deputy."

"He told me you don't want to file a formal complaint or press charges."

"That's correct."

"May I ask why? It's obvious your property has been damaged, and we were able to identify the owner of the vehicle."

"I don't think there's any point."

Twin grooves appeared on his brow. "I'm not sure I follow you."

"Let it go, Sheriff." Her eyes went flat.

The grooves deepened. "Ms. Turner, my job is to see that justice is done. When a wrong has been committed, I try to correct it. In this case, that would be very easy to do—with your cooperation."

The brim of her hat shadowed her eyes—but not enough to hide the brief flash of cynicism that flickered in their depths. "Right."

He folded his arms across his chest and gave her a speculative squint. "I'm not sure what that means. But if you won't press charges on your own behalf, look at it this way. Up until now, Stephen Mueller's worst crime has been joy riding and property damage. However, you were close enough to read the license plate this morning. That means you could have been killed. The next time this happens, the witness might be. Do you really want that hanging over your head?"

"I'm not responsible for other people's behavior, Sheriff." She held her ground, trying not to let his perceptive gaze drill past her walls. Nor let the guilt he was dishing out sway her resolve.

She was tough, he'd give her that, Dale conceded. Whatever her reasons, she wasn't backing down. He took a step closer, noting the sudden whitening of her knuckles as she tightened her grip on the handle of the shovel, the flash of fear that swept across her face. He stopped several feet away, stymied.

"Look, Les Mueller, the owner of the car, is a decent man trying to cope with a rebellious adolescent. Stephen is a good kid at heart, but he's making some mistakes. I'd like to get them corrected before he finds himself in real trouble."

When his comment produced no response, Dale sighed and propped his hands on his hips. "Okay, could you at least explain why you think filing a complaint would be pointless?"

After a brief hesitation, she responded. "I understand the owner of the vehicle is a man of some importance in town."

"That's true." Dale watched her, gauging her reactions, hoping this was leading to an explanation that made sense.

"Powerful people do what they want. And get away with it."

"Not in this town."

She responded with a silence and a cynical expression.

Indignation tightened Dale's jaw, and his eyes narrowed almost imperceptibly. "For the record, that's not the way things work here. We prosecute crimes and do our best to see that the injured party receives restitution."

"With people in power, retribution is more likely than restitution." Her face hardened, and acrid bitterness etched her words.

A few seconds of silence ticked by while his unrelenting gaze bore into hers. When he spoke, his voice was quiet. "Why would you think that?"

His question seemed to startle her. She took an involuntary step back. Swallowed. Blinked. "I'm not going to press charges, Sheriff. No matter what you say."

The finality in her tone told Dale he'd lost his argument. And her sudden pallor suggested she was once again afraid. The question was, why? Dale didn't have a clue. Nor was he likely to find out, he acknowledged, given the stubborn tilt of her chin.

"If you change your mind, don't hesitate to call."

"I'll keep that in mind."

Her dismissive inflection suggested she'd do the exact opposite. That she wouldn't spare it another thought once he walked away. But he'd given it his best shot, offered his most persuasive argument. In the end, it was her call.

Switching gears, he summoned up a smile. "On a different subject, thank you for the picture book. It came this morning. It wasn't necessary, but Jenna will love it."

There was a warmth in his tone as he spoke his daughter's name, a subtle softening of his features. Christine's own manner thawed a fraction of a degree. "I'm glad. It's hard to go wrong with a book about a princess for a little girl that age."

"It was right on. Our current nightly story-time ritual alternates between *Cinderella* and *Sleeping Beauty*. I could recite the books in my sleep at this point."

A sheriff who read his child bedtime stories. Surprising. But nice. "I'm sure her mom feels the same way."

A brief shadow darkened his eyes, like a cloud passing in front of the sun. "Her mother died when she was eighteen months old."

Shock rippled across Christine's features. "I'm sorry."

"Thanks. My mom has stepped in to help, and that's been a great blessing." He nodded toward the torn-up garden. "If you have a change of heart about reporting this incident, let me know."

With that, he turned and strode back toward his car.

Long after he left, Christine stood in the middle of

her topsy-turvy pumpkin patch, thinking about the motherless little girl who called the sheriff "Dad." Her own situation had been similar but reversed. Her father had died when she was six, before she'd formed any clear memories of him. But her mother had tried her best to compensate for the loss.

All her life, Christine had known that her mother would do anything, sacrifice anything, for her. She'd been loved with such deep devotion that nothing later in life could take away the foundation of self-worth her mother had laid. That foundation had held her in good stead through the hard times, allowing her to retain her self-esteem even as Jack had done his best to destroy it.

For some reason, Christine had a feeling that Jenna would grow up with the same solid foundation of confidence and dignity. Christine might not trust Dale Lewis as a sheriff, but she knew at some intuitive level that he was a loving, devoted father. And that if Jenna could have only one parent, she was lucky to have him.

There was a time, in a situation like this, when Christine would have uttered a silent prayer in her heart, asking the Lord to protect the little girl and to give her father strength to carry on alone. But she didn't talk much to the Lord anymore. In her time of need He'd let her down, and her once-solid faith had faltered. Now, she regarded prayer as no more likely to yield results than standing in the middle of a pumpkin patch wishing for a fairy godmother to appear.

And as for Prince Charming… It was a whole lot safer to leave him in the pages of a fairy tale.

Chapter Four

"And they lived happily ever after. The End." Dale closed the book and smiled at Jenna. Snuggled beneath the covers, her golden hair splayed on the pillow, his daughter exuded an innocence and unbridled enthusiasm that was a balm to his soul.

"I like that story, Daddy. Can I be a princess when I grow up?"

"You're my princess right now, sweetie." He reached over and tickled her, enjoying her giggles as she squirmed away from him.

"I mean a princess with a crown and a pretty long dress and a happy ending, like the reluc...lucant princess in the book."

"You can be anything you want to be, honey." Soon enough, the world would teach her that happy endings were often confined to storybooks. He wasn't going to be the one to disillusion her.

"Tell me again how you met the lady who sent me this book today."

For some reason, Jenna was fascinated by the tale of Christine and Dale's encounter.

"It was rainy outside, and the road was slippery. Her car slid off the edge of the blacktop and she hit her head, so I took her to see Dr. Martin. She sent the book to say thank you."

"Then you rescued her, just like the prince in the book rescued the reluctant princess?"

"Well, there weren't any dragons around. But I did help her. That's what policemen do. They help people who are in trouble."

"What does she look like?"

An image of Christine popped into his mind, the way she'd looked in the pumpkin patch this afternoon, with a streak of dirt across her forehead. "She has brown eyes—kind of soft and velvety, like the cattails we saw at the lake, remember?—and her hair is brownish-red and wavy, and it touches her shoulders."

"Is she pretty?"

Dale pictured the gentle curve of her cheek, her thick fringe of lashes, the delicate jaw and soft, full lips. Not to mention the well-shaped legs outlined beneath her snug jeans, or the way she was softly rounded in all the right places. Oh, yeah, she was pretty. No living, breathing male could fail to notice that.

"Yes, honey, she's pretty."

"I wish I could meet her."

His daughter's wistful tone tugged at Dale's heart. "She has a farm and she's very busy. But we might see her in town sometime."

"Is she a mommy?"

"I don't think so, honey. She's kind of a mystery lady."

A frown creased Jenna's brow. "What does that mean?"

"It means no one knows very much about her. But I think she lives by herself." He'd seen no ring on her finger to suggest she had an equally reclusive husband.

"I bet she gets lonesome."

Did she? Dale wondered. If so, she wasn't doing anything to rectify the situation. The question was, why not? She was a young woman. Surely she yearned on occasion for companionship. For love. As he did.

A faint pang of melancholy stirred in Dale's heart, like the indistinct outer ripples after a stone is dropped in the water. Over the years, the sharp pain of loss had dissipated. But the dull ache never went away. Despite the problems in his marriage, he missed sharing his life with one special person.

Oh, he had Jenna and his mother. And plenty of friends. But it wasn't the same as being in a loving, committed relationship. Friends and family didn't ease the loneliness of the dark nights when he lay awake yearning for the comfort of a warm embrace, a whispered endearment, the sense of peace that had filled him when his wife had lowered her defenses long enough to sleepily snuggle against him as he gathered her in his arms.

Those moments had been rare, but he'd cherished them. And he missed them.

"Daddy." Jenna tugged on his sleeve, calling him back to the present. "Do you think the mystery lady gets lonesome?"

"I don't know, honey. Maybe."

"We could visit her."

Not a good idea. Christine had made it clear she didn't welcome contact with the sheriff's department. "We'll see, honey."

"That means no." Disappointment flooded Jenna's face. Like most five-year-olds, she knew how to interpret that response. "Don't you like her?"

Frankly, Dale didn't know how he felt about Oak Hill's newest resident. She intrigued him. He found her attractive. He was curious about her past. But as for liking her…

"I don't know her very well, Jenna. You can't decide if you like someone until you get to know them."

"I can tell right away if I like somebody," his daughter declared.

That might be true, Dale conceded. Children approached strangers with an open mind, while adults' pasts colored new relationships.

"That's because you're such a smart little girl." Dale leaned over and kissed Jenna's forehead. Standing, he set the book on her nightstand. "Sleep tight, sweetie."

"You, too, Daddy. I think I'll dream about the reluctant princess. And the mystery lady."

"That sounds good. You can tell me all about it at breakfast tomorrow."

Shutting the door halfway, Dale headed for the kitchen. The two-bedroom bungalow was quiet as he opened the fridge and retrieved a soda, the only sound the hiss of carbonation as he flipped the tab. An odd restlessness plagued him, and he wandered over to the window and stared out into the darkness as he took a long swallow of his drink.

Jenna's interest in Christine, a woman she'd never met, seemed excessive. But in the past few months, his daughter had been asking more questions about her mother. And on several occasions she'd told him she wished she had a mommy like the other kids at the preschool she attended three mornings a week.

In truth, Dale wished she did, too. A one-parent household wasn't ideal. His mom did a great job filling in, and Jenna loved her fiercely, but it wasn't the same as having a mother in the house.

Perhaps Jenna thought Christine might be a candidate for the job. It wouldn't be the first time she'd broached the subject, Dale mused, a wry smile tugging at his lips. To his embarrassment, she'd begun pointing out potential candidates at church— none of whom were suitable for a variety of reasons.

He'd put Christine in that category as well. She might be single and available, but there was an angst in her eyes, a deep-seated hurt and wariness, that reminded him too much of Linda. He wasn't about to go there again.

If Jenna wanted to dream about her, that was fine.

But he intended to walk a wide berth around her, both in his dreams *and* in his life.

The crunch of gravel announced the approach of a visitor, and Christine shaded her eyes and looked down her drive toward the road. An unfamiliar car was closing the distance between them, but at least it was unmarked, she noted in relief. For a second she'd been afraid the sheriff was repeating his visit of the previous day.

Stripping off her gloves, she rose from her kneeling position and removed her hat. As the car came to a stop she headed toward it, passing row after row of healthy herbs. She'd have a good supply for the next farmers' market, she thought in satisfaction.

As she approached the drive, three women alighted. She recognized Marge at once, in her hot-pink tunic top. Cara Martin's distinctive red hair glinted in the sun. The third woman was unfamiliar.

"Christine!" The iridescent beading on Marge's top shimmered as she gave an enthusiastic wave. "I hope you don't mind some visitors."

"And I hope you don't mind a little dirt." Christine brushed at the knees of her jeans and pushed her hair back from her face, leaving a streak of grime on her cheek.

"The sign of a working farmer," Marge declared. "Christine, you've met Cara. This is Abby Warner-Campbell. Abby used to be the editor of our *Gazette*. Now she's the editorial director for Campbell Publishing in Chicago, which acquired the *Gazette* about a year ago. But she and her husband get back to Oak Hill on a regular basis. She stopped by the inn to visit, and when she heard about our excursion she invited herself along."

Abby moved forward and extended her hand. "Just a nose for news, I guess. I thought your farm might make a nice feature for the *Gazette* and I wanted to check it out before passing the idea on to the editor."

"Some publicity would be great for business. Thanks for your interest." Christine returned the woman's firm handshake.

"I brought some homemade oatmeal cookies." Marge held up a tin. "I was hoping to bribe you for a tour."

"No bribe necessary. I'll be glad to show you around."

"Wonderful! Let me set these cookies on the porch." Marge trotted across the stone walk toward Christine's two-story frame farmhouse and deposited the tin on a table.

Once Marge rejoined them, Christine led the way to the gardens. "There's not a lot to see yet, but I'll show you what I have and tell you my plans."

As they strolled between the neat rows, Christine

pointed out the sections devoted to oregano, sage, rosemary, basil, thyme, chives and various other herbs.

"I also grow organic flowers," she explained as they looked over row after row of colorful zinnias, wispy cosmos, sturdy snapdragons, spiky salvia and a dozen other varieties. "The bouquets have been big sellers at the farmers' markets. I'm developing a perennial garden, too—poppies, peonies, coneflowers, coreopsis, daisies." Christine gestured toward a section that was beginning to fill out. "And over there—" she pointed to a third parcel "—I've planted blackberries, strawberries and raspberries. Next year I'll begin harvesting them."

"Wow." Cara scanned the gardens as they completed the tour. "This is impressive, Christine. How much land do you have?"

"About eight acres. But I only cultivate a small portion. I hope to increase the size of the garden each year."

"It's pretty large now, if you ask me. How do you manage to tend it all yourself?"

"I spend every minute of daylight out here. But I love it."

"Is this your first venture into organic gardening?" Abby asked.

"Yes. On this scale, anyway. But I've always loved gardening. That and books are my passion."

"Are you a big reader?" Marge queried, not one to be left out of a conversation for too long.

"Yes. In fact, I was a librarian for many years."

"Is that right?" Marge's expression grew thoughtful. "I'll have to mention that to Eleanor Durham. She's looking for someone to help out at the library two days a week, now that Sally Boshans and her husband are retiring to Florida."

"I don't know, Marge." Cara looked over the garden again, her expression dubious. "This is more than a full-time job."

"Well, cooler weather will be here soon. Christine can't garden then. Maybe she could fill in here and there until Eleanor lines up someone else." Marge leaned over and patted Christine's hand. "Think about it, dear. I'll have Eleanor call you."

"I, for one, came out here to buy some herbs," Cara declared. "And I want some flowers for the tables at the restaurant, too. Are you open for business?"

Christine smiled. "I never pass up a sale."

While the two of them returned to the garden, Marge retreated to the shade of the porch, fanning herself and pilfering a few cookies as she chatted with Abby. After Cara finished shopping, Abby peppered Christine with more questions. Although Christine didn't reveal anything that wasn't public knowledge, the three visitors found out more in forty-five minutes than anyone else had learned in almost three months.

"So do you have any family left in Nebraska?" Marge asked as the women stowed Cara's purchases in the car.

"No. My dad died when I was six, and I didn't have any siblings. My mom died of Alzheimer's six months ago."

"A terrible disease," Marge sympathized. "And losing your husband a year ago, at such a young age…I had no idea. But you picked a good place to start over. The folks in Oak Hill are the salt of the earth. I came here from Boston a few years back after inheriting the inn, and they welcomed me with open arms. They'll do the same for you, too, if you give them a chance."

She tilted her head and regarded Christine. "You know, one good way to meet people is to attend Sunday services. We always have a coffee hour afterward and everyone stays to chat. You'd be welcome to join us. It's the church with the big white steeple in the middle of town."

No thank you, Christine thought, suppressing a shudder. It had been almost two years since she'd gone to church by choice. She'd attended her mother's and Jack's funerals, of course. And she'd accompanied her husband to services when he'd insisted her presence at his side was necessary for his image. The recollection of standing beside him in the house of God while he pretended to be a Christian still sickened her. Going back would only call up those memories, in all their vivid repugnance.

Besides, God hadn't been there for her when she'd needed Him most. Why should she visit Him now?

But she didn't give voice to any of those thoughts. Her relationship with the Lord was her own business. She simply thanked Marge for the invitation, said her goodbyes and went back to work as the car crunched down the driveway toward the main road.

For some reason, though, the older woman's invitation kept echoing in her mind. Despite the wall she'd built between herself and the Lord, deep inside a part of her missed attending a worship service every week and reading her neglected Bible. For most of her life, she'd found comfort and courage and solace in her faith.

Even while things deteriorated with Jack, she'd maintained her relationship with the Lord, seeking His help and guidance. Trapped in an intolerable situation, she'd prayed for His intervention. Begged for release, for a way out. But months had passed with no response.

At first, Christine had told herself there must be a reason God had allowed her to become trapped in a nightmare. That conviction had sustained her, as she'd examined—and discarded—every possible explanation. At that point, she'd tried to convince herself that despite the unfairness of the situation, the indignities she'd suffered had been worth it. That her misery had ensured the best possible care for her mother. Had been the *only* way to ensure that care.

She knew that for a fact. She'd tried the only other option she could think of. After that had failed, she'd reminded herself that she could never do enough to repay her mother for all her sacrifices, for all the years she'd cleaned office buildings and taken in ironing to give her daughter security and an education. Told herself that she was strong enough to hold on as long as her mother needed her.

The concept of repaying that debt had helped Christine endure the humiliation and terror and abuse. But eventually, to her shame, she'd begun to resent her mother. Toward the end, as she'd sat in the room at the extended-care facility, no longer recognized by the woman who'd borne her, she'd even begun to wish for her mother's death. All the things that had made Helen Turner a unique individual—her intellect, her spirit, her capacity to love—had been stripped away, leaving nothing but a physical body. A body Christine could only sustain by living a nightmare.

In the end, Jack's sudden death had liberated her. But it had been too late to salvage her withered faith, to dispel the bitterness she felt toward the God who had abandoned her.

She knew her situation wasn't unique. The Bible was filled with stories about holy men and women who had endured worse than she had. But she hadn't dwelt on the injustice of it until it had happened to her. After it had, she'd been unable to comprehend how God could allow His faithful followers to suffer. She hadn't understood why He would let her be tortured to sustain an empty shell that would never again be filled.

But Christine had understood one thing.

There was no room in her life for an uncaring God.

By late that afternoon, Christine was ready for a work break. She straightened up and flexed her back, thinking that a cold drink was in order. It might be mid-September, but the Missouri heat was relentless. The consistent mideighties temperatures, plus the high humidity, could sap energy as effectively as a puncture could flatten a tire. Christine had come close to dehydration on a couple of occasions, and she'd learned to drink more water. Now she kept a large Thermos close by, refilling it throughout the day.

As she pulled off her gloves and headed to the end of the row where she'd propped her Thermos, she noticed a car slowing at her driveway for the third time in two days. Not an official vehicle, thank goodness, but one that was familiar—and that caused her pulse to accelerate.

It was the same car that had skidded through her roadside garden yesterday.

Her stance tense and wary, she watched the car slow by her pumpkin patch as it traversed the drive. It stopped near her front door, and two people emerged—a man with sun-streaked light brown hair who looked to be in his early forties, and the blond-haired teen she'd caught sight of yesterday as the car had careened across her property.

As the older man started toward her porch he said

something over his shoulder that Christine couldn't hear, and the teen followed with obvious reluctance.

It had to be Les Mueller and his son, Stephen. But why were they here? She'd filed no complaint, caused them no trouble. Nor did she plan to. In fact, she wanted nothing to do with them.

Since they hadn't yet noticed her, she considered retreating to the back of the house, where she could take refuge in one of the outbuildings until they left. On the other hand, why hide? It was broad daylight. She was within view of the road and passing cars. It was her property. There was no reason to be afraid.

Straightening her shoulders, she wiped her hands on her jeans and headed in their direction.

As she approached, the older man noticed her. He put his hand on the teen's shoulder, inclined his head her way and strode toward her, waiting to speak until he was a few feet away. The young man followed in his wake.

"Ms. Turner?"

"Yes."

He extended his hand. "Les Mueller."

Realizing that nervousness had dampened her palm, Christine once more wiped it on her jeans before taking his hand. The man's callused grip was firm, and he had blue eyes, like the sheriff, she noted. Except this man's were the color of a pale summer sky, while Dale Lewis's were as deep blue as a pure mountain lake. The dairy owner's weathered face suggested he'd spent too many hours in the sun, and his firm, no-nonsense chin belonged to a man who didn't tolerate foolishness. Dressed in jeans, boots and a cotton shirt rolled to the elbows, he needed only a brimmed hat to look every bit a cowboy.

Without waiting for Christine to acknowledge his self-introduction, he spoke again. "I understand my son was responsible for some damage to your property yesterday."

Anger bubbled up inside her. It seemed the sheriff had ignored her wishes and had taken matters into his own hands, going behind her back after she'd refused to press charges. Now, thanks to him, she'd provoked the ire of the town's leading citizen. She could see his displeasure in the tense lines of his face. Her heart skipped a beat, and she edged back a step.

"I didn't file a formal complaint."

"That's what Dale said. He told me what happened, off the record. I'm glad he did. The way I understand it, not only did my son damage one of your gardens, he came close enough to hit you. That kind of behavior shouldn't go unpunished. But the first order of business is an apology. Stephen?"

The man stepped aside, planted his hands on his hips and looked at his son. The boy turned beet-red, and he jammed his hands in his pockets, staring at the ground as he spoke. "I'm sorry about the damage."

Tilting her head, Christine studied him, a slight frown marring her brow as she played the incident back in her mind. She seemed to recall that a black-haired kid had been at the wheel. "You weren't driving the car, were you?"

The boy's ruddy color deepened and he risked a quick peek at his father as he mumbled a response. "No, ma'am."

"You let someone else drive?" Les's eyes narrowed, and fury nipped at the edges of his voice.

From his outraged tone, Christine deduced that this was another, unreported transgression.

"Yes, sir."

"Who?"

"Eric."

Expelling an exasperated breath, Les jammed his fingers through his short-cropped hair. "You know the rules, Stephen. No one drives the car but you."

"Yes, sir. I know." The boy shuffled one toe in the dirt and hung his head. "But it was his birthday, and he said he'd always wanted to drive a Lexus. I didn't think it would hurt to let him drive for a mile or two. I didn't know he was going to take off like a bat out of…" He stopped short when his father cleared his throat. "Anyway, I told him to go slower. But he didn't pay any attention. I'm sorry."

"It seems you have a lot to be sorry for." Les's curt response didn't cut his son any slack. Angling back toward Christine, the man added his own apology. "I'm embarrassed by the behavior of my son. He's young, but that's no excuse for irresponsibility. I hope you'll find it in your heart to forgive him. And we'd both like to make amends."

With a start, Christine realized that the anger she'd detected in the man was directed at his son, not her. She sensed nothing in his manner but sincerity as he apologized. Relief coursed through her, and her rigid stance relaxed a fraction.

"The apology is accepted, and there's no need to make amends."

"Yes, there is. I want you to know that my son's driving privileges have been revoked. Originally for a month, but now for two, given his mistake with Eric." He spared his son a quick look, and the boy's color once again surged. "I'd also like to compensate you for damages. It appears to me you've lost about half your pumpkin crop. Come October, that will translate to a significant amount of money."

He mentioned a figure, and Christine's eyes widened. She shook her head in protest. "That's far too much."

"Not after you factor in the sweat equity that went into creating the garden. Not to mention the salvage operation."

Put that way, it was hard to argue with the man's rationale, Christine admitted.

"And I'd like to send Stephen over here to put in a little sweat equity of his own."

Turning her attention to the teen, Christine surveyed the lanky youth. In all honesty, she wouldn't mind some assistance with the physical work. The labor-intensive nature of organic farming was proving to be a bit more taxing than she'd expected. She'd always known that if she wanted to expand, she'd have to bring in some part-time help. But she hadn't planned to take that step this year. Besides, the last thing she wanted on her hands was a teenager with an attitude.

"I appreciate the offer, Mr. Mueller, but that's not necessary."

"It's Les. We country folk aren't much into formality." He gave her a brief, engaging grin, and she was struck by his down-to-earth manner. How different he was from Jack, Christine thought. As the leading citizen of Dunlap, Nebraska, her husband had always made it a point to find subtle ways to remind people of the power he wielded—including an insistence on being addressed as "mister."

Nor had he had any qualms about abusing his position. Had he found himself in a position like Les Mueller, he would never have humbled himself as the dairy owner had done, nor would he have behaved with such integrity in trying to right a wrong. It was nice to know there were a few honorable people in positions of importance in small towns.

"My wife and I would appreciate it if you'd take Stephen on, Ms. Turner."

"Christine."

He acknowledged her correction with a smile and

a slight nod. "The only way to learn from mistakes is to pay the consequences. Stephen's a good worker, and he's available after school and on weekends. I figure forty hours of labor ought to cover it. And keep him out of trouble for the foreseeable future."

Once again, Christine was taken aback. Forty hours translated to a huge commitment for a teenager who was also juggling school, homework and extra-curricular activities.

"I'm not sure we could work that off before I close down the farm for the winter," she pointed out.

"I realize that. Anything left over can be carried into the spring."

It was clear that Les had thought this through. And she couldn't fault his intentions. In theory, people should pay the consequences for their actions. She just hadn't seen that principle enforced very often over the past couple of years. Yet she didn't want to have to deal with some sullen teen who was intent on making her life miserable.

Uncertain, she directed her next comment to Stephen. "Do you know anything about organic farming?"

"No, ma'am. But I'm willing to learn. And I'm pretty good with a shovel."

"How do you feel about working here?"

For the first time, he looked her straight in the eye. "It's not the way I planned to spend my fall. But I figure it's fair. What I did was wrong. And like the sheriff said, it could have been a whole lot worse if...if the car had hit you." He swallowed hard. "I figure I was lucky. That maybe this was God's way of telling me to shape up before I really mess things up. Digging in the dirt will give me a chance to get my act together."

Surprised by his mature response, Christine was forced to revise her opinion of the teen. She'd expected him to be belligerent and resentful. Instead, he'd accepted responsibility for his actions and was receptive to his father's plan. How could she turn him down?

"Okay. We'll give it a try," Christine capitulated, folding her arms across her chest. "Can you come by after school tomorrow?"

"He'll be here," Les answered for his son. Holding out his hand, he took Christine's in a parting grip. "Thank you for your understanding. I'll put that check in the mail to you tonight."

"I'll see you tomorrow, Ms. Turner." Stephen reached out to her as well. Like his father, he had a firm grip. But unlike the older man, his hand was free of calluses, the skin soft and unused to physical labor. That wouldn't last long once he began working at the farm, though. Even with gloves, it was hard to avoid blisters. Christine's own work-roughened hands attested to that. This kind of labor toughened you up, made you appreciate the effort required to reap a high-quality, bountiful harvest.

And she had a feeling that was exactly what Stephen's father hoped would happen with his son.

As Christine watched the car disappear in a cloud of dust down the gravel driveway, she took a drink of water from her Thermos, letting the cool liquid soothe her parched throat. It seemed the sheriff had been correct when he'd told her that Les Mueller would want to make things right. And she appreciated the dairy owner's integrity.

What she didn't appreciate was Dale Lewis's interference. Yes, everything had turned out fine. But it could have had a far worse ending if Les had a different personality. One like Jack's, for example. One that would have compelled him to punish her in retaliation for causing problems. And she didn't want to go there. Not ever again.

That's why she steered clear of the folks in Oak Hill. If she didn't mingle, there wasn't any risk. She wanted nothing to do with the small-town politics and power plays. She was perfectly content to tend her farm and keep to herself.

But since the night of her accident, things had changed. She'd had a series of visitors, and she'd met more people in the past dozen or so days than she had in the entire first two months of her stay in Missouri. Most had seemed nice. But she'd learned the hard way that a friendly demeanor could mask a hidden agenda.

And that brought her back to Dale Lewis. On the

surface, he, too, seemed nice enough. But why had he ignored her wishes and reported the incident to Les? Was it because he hated to let injustice go unpunished, as he'd implied? Or was there some other motive? Had he done it to spite her, to incite her anger? Was it a vindictive response to her refusal to take his advice to press charges?

Christine didn't know. Nor did she need to. This situation had worked out fine, thank goodness. And there wouldn't be another. Now that she understood how the sheriff operated, she wouldn't give him the opportunity to thwart her again. Nor any reason to single her out for special attention.

Because the less she had to do with local law enforcement, the safer she'd be.

Chapter Five

Feeling guilty, Dale tapped his index finger on his desk and stared at his computer screen. He had no reason to run a background check on Christine Turner. No official reason, anyway. And never, since day one in his career as a cop, had he delved into files looking for information on someone who wasn't part of an investigation. He'd always considered it an invasion of privacy. Always believed that his access to both public and confidential data was a privilege that shouldn't be abused. That hadn't changed.

Yet here he was, on the verge of checking out the owner of Fresh Start Farm. Why?

Perturbed, Dale glanced out the window of his office at old Widow Harper's colorful flower bed next door. Every summer, she tended her zinnia garden. And every fall, like clockwork, she put a circle of mums around her front lamppost. With her bun of soft white hair and her pink face, she looked the same today as she had when he was a kid. Her expression was always kind and gentle, her manner the same. She was what she seemed.

But years and experience had taught Dale that such wasn't always the case. Many people kept their true identities hidden, guarded secrets, were less than honest. Sometimes that behavior was driven by fear, sometimes by a desire to take advantage of others. But whatever the motivation, he'd learned to trust his instincts. When a warning flag went up, he paid attention and approached with caution.

And Christine Turner's odd behavior had set a red flag waving. While there could be a lot of reasons why a person might be jittery around a police officer, the most obvious one was that he or she had something to hide. The fact that Christine also kept to herself, diligently avoiding social interaction, further aroused his suspicions.

Telling himself he needed to check her out just to be sure she wasn't a threat to the community, Dale leaned forward and initiated a search through the FBI's National Crime Information Center.

Ten minutes later, he'd come up blank. There was no police record in the national database for anyone named Christine Turner.

Switching gears, he zeroed in on Nebraska. According to Marge, who'd paid Oak Hill's newest resident a couple of visits, that was her home state. Perhaps a more concentrated search would yield results.

The localized approach took a bit longer, but it turned up a wealth of data. Christine Turner had been born thirty-five years ago in Omaha. She'd graduated with honors from both high school and college, earning a degree in library science. After finishing school, she'd worked for eight years as a librarian in Omaha before marrying a Jack Barlow. Her residence had then switched to Dunlap. After her husband died a year ago, she'd taken back her maiden name. Unusual, but not illegal, Dale mused.

Now that he had a married name, he did another search through the crime databases. And this time he hit pay dirt.

In the final year of her husband's life, she'd received numerous tickets and citations from the Dunlap police. They ran the gamut from simple parking and speeding violations to charges of reckless driving, resisting arrest and DUI. At one point, her license had been revoked for six months. The records also indicated she'd spent the night in the local jail on one occasion.

A troubled frown marring his brow, Dale closed out the search. The police record couldn't be discounted, but something about it didn't feel right. He couldn't imagine the wary woman with the soft brown eyes as a lawbreaker.

For one thing, the pieces didn't fit. He'd seen Christine a few times since the night of her accident. From a distance, when she didn't know she was being observed. Twice in town, once on the state highway. In Oak Hill, she drove with caution and prudence, making full stops at the stop signs, signaling as she turned, slowing for pedestrians…even for dogs. On the highway, she'd driven at a moderate rate of speed, dead center in the lane, her gaze alert and fixed on the road.

A stray parking ticket Dale could buy. It happened to the best, most conscientious drivers on occasion. But speeding or reckless driving? He'd seen no evidence of that.

As for resisting arrest…he thought back to the night of the accident, how he'd rounded the cab and found her clutching a piece of wood, fear coursing through her glazed eyes as she struggled to remain upright. Had he tried to arrest her, he had a feeling she'd have resisted mightily. But she hadn't done anything wrong. Why had she been afraid he might try?

Unless she'd been drinking. He'd wondered about alcohol that night, given her peculiar reaction to him. After his years in L.A., he was well versed in the destructive nature of alcohol abuse. He'd seen how overindulgence could cause a normally responsible person to behave in an erratic, reckless manner.

But he'd smelled no liquor on her breath, nor found any evidence of alcohol in her truck. Still, drinkers had a way of hiding their addiction. And living alone, out in the country, would provide her with the perfect opportunity to drink unobserved, if she chose to.

Yet he found the whole notion of a DUI charge hard to swallow. Christine Turner didn't strike him as the heavy-drinker type. She worked hard, judging from what he'd seen of her farm on his one visit. She'd thrown herself into the monumental task of starting a new, labor-intensive business, toiling from sunup to sundown, if Marge was to be believed. Someone with a serious alcohol problem wasn't likely to have the focus or energy or drive to take that on.

Perhaps, though, she'd had a problem in the past, Dale speculated. The day they'd met, he'd recognized the look in Christine's eyes, which had echoed the expression he'd often seen in his wife's. A look that told him Christine had endured some kind of trauma that continued to color her perceptions of the world. Alcohol could be her way of coping with that hurt.

Linda, too, had needed a way to cope, but she'd struggled with bulimia—an ongoing battle Dale had prayed every day that she'd win. And those prayers had seemed to reap results in their last few months together. It always struck him as ironic that just as she'd seemed to turn a corner with her problem, her life had been cut short.

As for Christine—Dale hoped she'd succeed in subduing whatever demons plagued her existence. If the name of her farm was any indication, she was certainly making an all-out effort to start over. And he wished her well. Because if her past was anything like Linda's, it would be a long, hard, uphill fight.

* * *

"Christine? This is Eleanor Durham. Marge said she mentioned to you a week or so ago that I might call. I'd like to talk with you about working a couple of days a week in our humble little library. Please call me at your convenience."

As Christine jotted down the number the woman had left on her answering machine, she shook her head. Marge was a dynamo, no question about it. Not only did she run the Oak Hill Inn and serve as president of the chamber of commerce, last year she'd convinced Cara Martin—a cordon bleu chef from Philadelphia— to open an upscale restaurant three nights a week at the inn. Cara had told her the story when she'd placed a second order by phone two days ago.

Abby was no slouch, either. Two days after the women had visited, Christine had received a call from the editor of the *Gazette*. A reporter and photographer had appeared the following day. The resulting feature story was scheduled to run in an upcoming edition of the weekly paper.

It seemed the whole town was invading her space. Including the sheriff. But she had to admit that his interference in the reckless driving incident had turned out to be a blessing in disguise. Like clockwork Stephen Mueller showed up three days a week after school and on Saturday afternoons. His muscle power had eased her workload quite a bit, and he'd exhibited a genuine interest in the farm, asking intelligent questions and showing a real knack for understanding the principles and practices of organic farming.

Considering her vow to lay low and maintain her distance from the townspeople, Christine found all this activity unsettling. Yet the human contact felt good. Her self-imposed isolation had given her a feeling of safety, but it had been lonely. She wasn't, by nature, a recluse. One of the things she'd loved about her library work was the opportunity to interact with a variety of people every day.

Now she was being offered the chance to return to that work on a part-time basis. And it was doable, she acknowledged. Three weeks ago, she wouldn't even have been able to consider it, given her workload. But the season was beginning to wind down. And since she could count on Stephen to not only show up but offer real assistance, she might be able to fit in a few hours a week at the library.

Deciding it couldn't hurt to talk with the woman, Christine tapped in her number. She recognized Eleanor's voice when she answered, and as soon as Christine identified herself the woman's enthusiasm crackled over the line.

"Oh, I'm so glad you called! I can't tell you how delighted I was when Marge said she'd found a real librarian who might be willing to fill in for Sally. Isn't she a wonder? She always says, 'Ask and you shall receive,' and she certainly does her part to make that happen. Can you imagine how hard it is to find a qualified librarian in a town the size of Oak Hill? Sally wasn't trained, you know, but she'd been here for years and learned a lot on the job. I'm devastated to lose her.

"But I've always believed that God provides—and now here you are! Marge told me how busy you are with the farm—it sounds very exciting, and I must get out there soon for a tour—but I hope you'll consider filling in, if only until I can round up someone else on a permanent basis."

By the time the woman stopped to take a breath, Christine was reeling from the effusive, nonstop download.

"I am busy," Christine confirmed. "But I also love library work. How much time would you need?"

"We're open Monday, Wednesday, Thursday and Saturday from ten until four. Sally always worked Monday and Thursday, but I'm very flexible. Right now I'm holding down the fort alone, and to be honest, much as I enjoy the library, it's cramping my style. I'm missing quality time with my two little grandbabies. Whatever you can manage would be much appreciated."

"I'm afraid I can't spare two days. I go to the farmers' market in St. James and Rolla on Tuesday, Friday and Saturday, and the day before I have to harvest and package my herbs and flowers. A few hours on Wednesday would work, and I could probably manage to cover the first three hours on Monday."

"Perfect! I can't tell you what a help this will be!"

"Would you like me to come in for an interview?"

"Oh, that's not necessary. I can tell from talking with you on the phone that you'll be fine." She mentioned a wage that seemed more than fair.

The woman must be desperate if she was willing to hire her sight unseen, Christine decided. "When would you like me to start?"

"How about next Monday?"

"That would be fine. But wouldn't you like some references, or perhaps a résumé?"

"Well, of course that would be very nice. Yes, I suppose we should have some documentation for our records. But if Marge says you'd be good for the job, that's enough for me. You can bring the résumé with you on Monday. You know where we are, don't you?"

On her occasional trips to town, Christine had noted the modest library, housed in a stand-alone building a few doors down from Dr. Martin's office. "Yes. I've driven by."

"Good. Then I'll see you Monday. I'll give you a tour—not that that will take long. I'm sure this is small potatoes compared to the library in Omaha. And I'll fill you in on our procedures, such as they are. You'll have it down in thirty minutes."

"I'll look forward to meeting you."

"Oh, the pleasure is all mine, trust me. Have a great weekend."

As the woman severed the connection, Christine

propped her chin in her hand and looked out the window beside her kitchen table. Stephen was still working in the herb garden, finishing up the day's harvesting. When he left, she'd put in another few hours of labor, sorting and packaging the herbs into small bunches and arranging the flowers in bouquets for the next day's trip to St. James. Now that she was a regular at the two area markets, she'd developed a growing base of steady customers, and more and more she was selling out well before the noon closing.

The farm was working out just as she'd hoped, she reflected in satisfaction. By next year, it would provide a welcome supplement to the income generated by the investments she'd made with her modest inheritance from Jack's estate. In the meantime, she was managing.

In retrospect, she supposed she should have fought for a bigger share of Jack's assets. For the sake of justice, if nothing else. After what he'd put her through, she'd deserved far more than he'd left her. But at the time of his death, she hadn't had the strength for it. She'd already been teetering on the verge of an emotional meltdown, her precarious mental state exacerbated by her mother's rapid deterioration. The thought of launching a legal battle she'd had no confidence she'd win had unnerved her.

Besides, as the attorney she'd consulted had pointed out, Jack had tied up all the loose ends, dotting all the *i*'s and crossing all the *t*'s. There was nothing to contest. The company, she'd discovered, had been left to a cousin, and most of Jack's other assets were linked to the business as well.

Once all the dust had settled, the house and some mutual funds had gone to her. She'd sold all the physical property at once, using the proceeds to buy Fresh Start Farm, and retained the investments for the small, steady income they provided. She was getting by, but the revenue from the farm would give her a little more breathing space.

"Ms. Turner? I took all the herbs to the packing shed. Do you need me for anything else today?"

Swallowing past the bitter taste in her mouth that thoughts of Jack always left, she turned toward the screen door and forced her lips into a smile. "No, thank you, Stephen. That should do it."

"Okay. I'll be back Saturday afternoon."

"Do you need to call your dad for a ride?"

The youth grinned. "Nope. He let me bring my cell phone today. I'm going to call Megan while I wait."

The cell phone had been one of his revoked privileges, and Megan was his girlfriend, Christine knew. He had shared quite a lot about his life as they worked side-by-side in the garden. And as she'd gotten to know him, she'd come to the same conclusion as the sheriff. He was a good kid at heart. A bit starry-eyed about this Megan, but she supposed that was the nature of young love. No dark clouds had yet moved in to dim those stars.

As she watched him stride down the drive to wait by the road, the phone to his ear, she was surprised by the sudden yearning that swept over her. A yearning to once again be young and in love. To believe in romance and happy endings. But experience had taught her the danger of trusting someone with her heart. She wouldn't make that mistake again.

In retrospect, Christine knew she'd been a victim of her own romantic fantasies when she'd met Jack five years ago, days after blowing out the candles on her thirtieth birthday cake with a wish for a little romance in her life. If an old school friend hadn't invited her at the last minute to accompany him to a dinner at the convention he was attending in Omaha, Christine would never have met the man who became her husband. It had seemed like fate.

The keynote speaker at the dinner, Jack had been the only son of a prosperous farm equipment dealer in out-state Nebraska. They'd exchanged no more than a few words, so she'd been surprised—and flattered—by his follow-up call. How could she have known that his ready smile and good looks masked a sadistic streak that would turn her life into a nightmare? Or that his promises on their wedding day had been empty? How could she have known he would find a way to trap her in an intolerable situation, or that his buddy, the local sheriff, would ignore her pleas for help?

Suppressing a shudder, Christine focused on

Stephen in the distance, deep in conversation with his girlfriend. Not all romances turned sour, she reminded herself. But if there was one Jack out there, there were others. And if she hadn't been able to see beneath her husband's veneer, she didn't trust herself to see beneath any man's.

With ruthless determination, she tamped down her sentimental yearnings. She didn't need romance or love in her life to be happy. She had her independence, not to mention Fresh Start Farm.

And that was enough.

As she finished the story and closed the book, Christine smiled at the six children seated cross-legged around her on the floor in one corner of the library. When she'd mentioned during her orientation tour with Eleanor that she used to do a children's story hour in Omaha, the older woman had enthusiastically embraced the idea.

Now, a week and a half into her part-time job, Christine had just conducted the first Oak Hill Library story hour. Judging by the animation on the young faces beaming up at her, it had been a resounding success.

"Can you read another one, Ms. Christine?" A freckle-faced little boy gave her a hopeful look. Brian, she recalled, from their earlier self-introductions.

After checking her watch, Christine shook her head. "Not today, Brian. I promised your mommies and grandmas that I'd be finished by two o'clock. But you can come again next week. And I have a treat for you before you leave. Wait here."

Rising, Christine retrieved a tin of homemade chocolate chip cookies from behind the counter in the middle of the single large room that housed the Oak Hill Library. Holding it up as she returned, she scanned the parents and grandparents who had accompanied the children, raising an eyebrow in query. At their nods, she passed the tin around, letting each child take a cookie. Then she offered them to the adults.

A young woman wearing far too much makeup gave her a shy smile as she took a cookie from the tin. "Thank you for starting this. Brian's only five, but he already loves books. He couldn't wait to come today."

"It's good to get children interested in books at a very young age. I'll never forget the first book I…"

A sudden bang interrupted their conversation. As Christine swiveled to check it out, the young mother gasped and gave a violent jerk, dropping her cookie.

"Sorry." The sheepish apology came from a patron across the room who had lost his grip on several books.

Giving him a reassuring smile, Christine turned back as the woman rose from retrieving her cookie. The color had drained from her cheeks, and a film of moisture beaded her upper lip. Concerned, Christine laid a hand on her arm, alarmed by the tremors beneath her fingertips. "Are you okay?"

The woman tucked a hank of limp blond hair behind her ear with a shaky hand. "Yeah. I'm fine."

But she didn't look fine. Now that her hair was pushed back, Christine could see a purple tinge on the skin stretched taut above her cheekbone, the bruise too discolored to be concealed even by the heavy makeup.

A sick feeling of dread clawed at Christine's stomach as her brain clicked into analytical mode. A facial bruise. Overreaction to the loud noise. The woman's attire. Despite the early October Indian summer weather, which had pushed temperatures back into the eighties, she wore a long-sleeved turtleneck that left little skin exposed.

The signs of abuse were all there.

"Mommy, can we come back next week?"

Little Brian drew their attention. Giving him a quick scan, Christine saw nothing to indicate he'd been touched. He wore a short-sleeved T-shirt and shorts, and the only marks on his face were his freckles.

"We'll try," the woman promised, taking his hand.

Christine wanted to stop her, to ask some questions, to offer help. She knew what it was like to be abused and alone. Jack hadn't hurt her physically—his abuse had been more sophisticated than that, and far less visible—but his sadistic behavior had left scars that sensitized her to this woman's plight. She couldn't let the young mother leave without at least getting her name.

"By the way, we haven't been formally introduced." She tried to keep her tone conversational as she held out her hand. "I'm Christine Turner."

"Erin Carson." The woman's handshake was tentative and quick. "We need to get home. Thank you again for today."

Before Christine could say anything else, the young mother led Brian toward the door.

"Now it's my turn to introduce myself."

Disturbed by her encounter with Erin, Christine shifted around to find a tallish woman with stylish white hair, hand extended.

"I'm Arlene Lewis. I brought my granddaughter, Jenna, today."

With a mental shake, Christine forced herself to switch gears and process this new information. Lewis. Granddaughter. Jenna. This must be the sheriff's mother. And the little blond-haired cherub with the blue eyes who'd sat at her feet for the past hour was his daughter.

Realizing that the woman was waiting for a return greeting, Christine took her proffered hand and forced her stiff lips into the semblance of a smile. The sheriff might make her nervous, but there was no reason to panic around his mother or child.

"It's nice to meet you."

"My pleasure. I understand you've met my son, the sheriff."

"Yes." She left it at that.

"It was so thoughtful of you to send the book to Jenna. Dale tells me that she insists he read it to her every night."

"I'm glad she liked it."

"And I'm glad we came today. I ran into Marge at a church meeting last night, and she said Eleanor had told her about the story hour. I knew Jenna would enjoy it. I told her when I picked her up from preschool at noon that I had a surprise for her, and she was almost too excited to eat lunch. Isn't that right, honey?"

The affection in Arlene's eyes as the little girl joined them, munching on her cookie, softened Christine's lips into a genuine smile.

"I ate some of my sandwich. And now I have dessert." She beamed as she held up the half-eaten cookie. "This is really good."

"I was just telling Ms. Christine how much you liked the book she sent to you."

The little girl's eyes widened. "Are you the mystery lady?"

Confused, Christine sent Dale's mother a questioning look. But the older woman seemed puzzled by the youngster's question, too.

"What do you mean, honey?" Arlene asked.

"Daddy said she's a mystery lady, because nobody knows very much about her."

"Oh, my. Little pitchers." Arlene gave Christine an apologetic look, then spoke to her granddaughter.

"Ms. Christine hasn't been in town very long. Pretty soon we'll all get to know a lot more about her."

"I already know she lives by herself. Daddy told me." Jenna tipped her chin up to regard Christine. "Don't you get lonesome?"

Taken aback by the candid question, Christine gave an honest, if incomplete, answer. "Well, I have a farm, so when I'm not here I'm pretty busy. I don't have much time to think about getting lonesome."

"That's what daddy said. And he said you were pretty. I think you're pretty, too."

Shaking her head, Arlene gave Christine a wry smile and took a firm grip on Jenna's hand. "I think it's time we said goodbye."

"Bye, Ms. Christine. I'll see you next week."

"Goodbye, Jenna.

The two made a quick exit. Christine watched through the window as the slightly stocky woman and the sprite of a little girl disappeared down the street in the direction of the sheriff's office. Were they going to pay him a visit and report that they'd met the "mystery lady"? Was Arlene going to alert her son that Jenna had passed on his compliment about Christine's appearance?

Christine wasn't sure how he'd respond to that news. But her own reaction was easy to identify. Surprise. She'd picked up nothing in the sheriff's manner to indicate he found her attractive. She'd sensed more suspicion and speculation than anything else. Yet according to his daughter, he'd said she was pretty.

Interesting, Christine mused as she returned to the counter.

And dangerous.

Which gave her one more excellent reason to avoid the sheriff.

Chapter Six

By the next Wednesday, the story group had increased to ten. Four newcomers had joined the original six children, all of whom had returned, including Brian and Jenna.

Once again Erin Carson was wearing a turtleneck. Christine had thought of her often during the preceding week, and she'd resolved that if Erin came today, she'd find some way to offer the woman assistance. Christine knew what it was like to be trapped in an intolerable situation with no ally. She didn't want anyone else to have to go through that.

Relief had surged through her when Erin and Brian had walked through the door. But it had been followed by trepidation when Jenna entered soon after, accompanied not by Arlene but by her father. The sheriff had nodded to her as they came in, and Jenna had waved. Christine had been too shocked to do more than gape at them. Why wasn't the sheriff at work? He was in uniform. Didn't he have anything better to do than take his mother's place at story hour?

Determined not to let his presence rattle her, Christine did her best to ignore him, focusing instead on the children's animated faces, relishing their enthralled attention during an adventure book and their unrestrained giggles after she switched to a humorous story. Children were such uncomplicated little creatures. And honest to a fault, as her conversation last week with Jenna had proven.

In fact, the child's indiscretion could be why the sheriff had accompanied her today, Christine realized. Perhaps he'd wanted to ensure that his daughter didn't let any other tidbits slip.

When Christine finished the books, she retrieved the treat for the day—sugar cookies. But instead of passing them out to the adults as she had at the last session, she set them on a table and invited the grown-ups to help themselves. As they congregated around the cookies, she drew Erin aside. Out of the corner of her eye she saw Dale cast a curious look in their direction, but she turned her back to him.

"Hello, Erin. I'm glad you came again." She smiled at the woman, relieved to see that the bruise on her cheek was fading and that she bore no visible evidence of new abuse.

"Brian's been waiting all week for today. But we can't stay." She cast a nervous glance toward the door. "My husband is on nights this week, and he needs the car. I dropped him off in the middle of town to run a few errands while we stopped in here. But I think we've stayed too long."

She looked past Christine and called out to Brian, motioning him to join her.

Her window of opportunity was closing fast, and Christine tried to think of some way to extend a hand of support without embarrassing the woman or making her uneasy.

"You know, I'm pretty new in town. I haven't met many people yet." She strove to keep her tone casual and conversational. "Maybe you could stop by my place sometime for a cup of coffee. I own Fresh Start Farm, not far from town. You might have seen the sign."

"Yes, I have." A flicker of interest flared in the woman's eyes, but it quickly dimmed. "I'd love to visit, but I don't think…"

The front door slammed open, and a burly man who looked close to forty, with brown hair a shade too long to be fashionable, pushed through. Scanning the room, his face settled into hard lines when he spotted Erin. "You're late."

The cold anger in his voice sent a chill down Christine's spine. And it seemed to have the same effect on Brian. The little boy tensed, melting against Erin under the protective arm she slipped around his shoulders.

"W-we were just leaving." Taking her son's hand, Erin started to move toward the man.

Christine restrained her for just a second with a

hand on her arm, and Erin's frightened gaze flew to hers. Christine pitched her voice low so only the young woman would hear her. "If you ever need help, call me."

"Erin."

At the threatening summons from her husband Erin pulled free and hurried toward him. When she drew close, he gripped her upper arm and propelled her toward the door. A second later, it whooshed shut behind the trio.

On the far side of the room, Dale swallowed the last bite of his cookie and brushed the sugar off his hands, his eyes narrowing as he processed the scene that had just transpired. He'd watched Christine seek out Erin Carson. Heard her invite the woman to visit, even though she avoided contact with everyone else in town. Seen her spine stiffen when Erin's husband grabbed his wife's arm. Sensed she'd wanted to intervene.

It was interesting that she had so quickly picked up the vibes between the Carsons, he reflected, as he strolled over to her. "The story hour was very nice. And the cookies are great."

His comment hung in the air for several moments before Christine angled toward him. And the pallor in her cheeks, the taut line of her lips, the concern in her eyes, confirmed that she'd detected a problem in the Carson family. And it had distressed her enough to compel her to break her self-imposed exile, to invite a stranger into her home. Why?

He couldn't ask that question, however. He needed to play this carefully. Christine Turner was not a woman who could be pushed. If he tried, she'd react like the sea anemones he used to find on the West Coast beaches, closing up when prodded.

The silence stretched between them, but at last she responded to his compliment. "Thanks."

"Homemade?"

"Yes."

"I'm surprised you have the time, with the farm and now the library job."

"I like to bake."

Since the conversation was going nowhere, Dale changed tactics. "Brian's a cute kid."

"Yes." A gust of worry wafted across her features.

"He's caught in a difficult situation." Folding his arms across his chest, he propped a shoulder against the end of a row of shelving.

She didn't pretend not to understand. Nevertheless, her expression was wary as she responded. "Erin had a bad bruise on her face last week."

"I've been called to the house several times by neighbors. Domestic violence is never pretty."

Her eyebrows rose a tiny fraction, as if she was surprised by his candor. "I suspected that might be the case. What's being done?"

"My hands are tied until Erin lodges a formal complaint or he touches Brian. So far he's left the boy alone."

"Physically, maybe. But what about the emotional and psychological damage?"

He sensed her frustration, and it matched his. He'd been down this road on plenty of occasions in L.A., sometimes with tragic outcomes. He'd always done his best to convince victims to press charges. But it took a lot of courage for a woman to stand up to an abuser. While he could put the weight of the law on Erin Carson's side, the courage to seek help had to come from within.

"I wish I could do more."

"How long has this been going on?"

"The Carsons moved here about eight months ago. I'm not sure where they came from. I got the first call a few weeks after they arrived. Derrick works as a laborer on a road crew. He's one tough character, and he's none too happy when I show up at the door."

"And I'll bet Erin pays for his displeasure later."

The bitterness in Christine's tone was so caustic, the pain and anguish in her unguarded eyes so intense, that Dale had a sudden, gut-clenching insight.

She's speaking from personal experience.

A muscle in his cheek clenched as he forced himself to take a long, slow breath. He'd suspected that Christine had been hurt, but until now he'd had no clue to the source of her trauma.

Struggling to maintain a placid facade despite the sudden churning in his gut, he spoke in a quiet voice. "Why would you think that?"

She blinked, regrouped, and her expression went neutral. "That seems to be the usual pattern, from what I've read."

"If she'd file an official complaint, I could get her out of there and issue a restraining order." He watched her, gauging her reaction, trying to bore through the curtain that had dropped over her face.

"Then something must be keeping her there."

"Like what?" After all the domestic violence calls he'd responded to, after all the homework he'd done on the subject, Dale still had a hard time grasping how a woman could allow herself to become a victim. Especially—if his instincts were correct—a woman like Christine, who seemed intelligent, independent and strong. The research he'd reviewed had cited any number of reasons women stayed in abusive relationships. And pointed out the risks to taking action. But weren't the risks of staying even greater?

Instead of answering his question, Christine looked away. "Only Erin could tell you that. Excuse me. I need to wrap things up here." Without giving him a chance to respond, she walked back to the group.

So much for trying to ferret out additional information. Frustrated, Dale jammed his fists into his pockets. Although she'd said nothing to confirm his suspicions, her reactions had been more than enough to disturb him. Yet the label of "battered wife" fit her no better than "lawbreaker." But it would explain why she'd taken back her maiden name after her husband's death, he conceded.

Not long ago, he'd told Jenna that Christine was a "mystery lady." It now appeared that his classification was more accurate than he'd realized. In fact, the mystery was thickening instead of resolving.

And if there was one thing a cop hated, it was an unsolved mystery.

Why Dale should care in this case eluded him, however. As far as Oak Hill was concerned, Christine Turner was a productive, law-abiding citizen. There was no reason for her to be on his radar screen.

Except for a pair of velvet brown eyes that harbored a hurt so deep it had somehow reached into his soul, awakened his protective instincts and stirred his heart to life.

That was the truth of it, Dale acknowledged. And while he might not like it, he never ran from the truth. For some reason, Christine had gotten under his skin. Despite his vow to walk a wide circle around problem-plagued women, she'd managed to breach his barriers. In the very act of pushing him away, she'd pulled him in.

Nevertheless, he didn't have to do anything about it. The safest course of action would be no action at all. Leave her to her self-imposed isolation and forget about her.

Yet as he watched her drop down to Jenna's level and engage his daughter in animated conversation, her expression warm, her defenses down, he found himself wishing she'd look at him like that.

With a sigh, Dale shook his head. He didn't need this complication in his life. Didn't *want* it in his life. But there it was. And he had no idea what to do about it.

Closing his eyes, Dale turned to the source of strength that never failed him.

Please, Lord, guide me through these murky waters. I'm not sure why You sent Christine here, but I don't want to get involved in another complicated relationship. The first one was hard enough. Yet I want to do Your will. If I'm supposed to help her in some way, show me how. But please help me protect my heart, too.

I ask also that You look with favor on Christine. Whatever her problems, I sense they're serious, and that she's deeply troubled. If she's not a believer, help her find her way home to You, the source of all goodness and hope. For only through You will she find peace. Amen.

A flash of lightning, followed by the sharp crack of thunder, confirmed the accuracy of the weather forecast. They were in for a storm.

Increasing his pressure on the accelerator, Dale hoped he'd make it to Christine's farm before the rain hit. Not that he wanted to be going there in the first place. He hadn't seen her since the story hour almost a week ago, and he wouldn't have sought her out today if the editor of the *Gazette* hadn't asked him to drop off some advance copies of the next issue, which featured the story about Fresh Start Farm.

Too bad he'd happened to mention he'd be patrolling in this area, Dale reflected. Unable to think of any logical reason to refuse the request, he'd agreed. But it didn't have to be a long visit. He'd drop the papers and go.

As he swung into her drive, the first few spatters of rain plopped onto his windshield, leaving trails down the glass like tears on a dusty face. In the distance, he saw Christine in the garden, hastily tossing bundles of greenery into two large baskets. Her back was to him, and she seemed oblivious to his approach.

Parking the car, he left the papers on the seat beside him and slid from behind the wheel. She was hurrying toward a shed behind the house, toting one of the baskets, and as Dale watched, a sudden, strong gust of wind rocked her. For an instant he thought she was going to lose her balance, but she righted herself and moved on, intent on her task.

The rain increased, and Dale jogged toward the remaining basket. Hefting it into his arms, he inhaled the pleasing, spicy scent of herbs as he strode toward the shed where Christine had disappeared. Though his burden wasn't heavy, the bulk made it awkward, and the boisterous wind seemed intent on tugging it from his arms.

He reached the shed door as Christine barreled out, narrowly avoiding a head-on collision by taking a quick step to the side. She gasped and reared back, clutching the door frame.

"Sorry. I saw you scampering to beat the rain as I pulled in and thought I'd lend a hand. I didn't mean to frighten you." Dale shifted the burden in his arms as larger drops of rain began to dissolve into dark splotches on his shirt.

Shooting a quick glance toward the ominous sky, Christine reached for the basket. "Thanks."

He tightened his grip. "Just tell me where you want it."

"Anywhere is fine." Christine stepped out of his way and motioned inside. "I need to get my tools." Brushing past him, she took off at a half run for the garden.

After setting the basket on the floor of the shed, Dale followed her. The rain was steady now, and the wind continued to increase as they gathered up the various implements strewn on the ground.

"I had my back to the storm. I didn't realize how bad it was until the first drops began to fall." The wind whipped Christine's breathless explanation from her lips as she bent to pick up the last trowel. "Okay, that's it. The toolshed's over there."

She gestured toward a smaller shed in the back of the house and hurried toward it, her head bent against the wind, her shirt already damp from the cool rain.

Ducking inside, she deposited the smaller garden

implements on the workbench while Dale leaned the shovel, three-pronged weeder and rake against the wall.

"Looks like it's going to be a bad one. I hope it doesn't escalate to…"

At the sudden bang behind him, Dale twisted to find that the door had blown shut. One tiny window beside the workbench provided a limited source of light, but with the heavy, dark storm clouds shrouding the sun, visibility in the shed was minimal.

In two steps Dale was beside the door. He pushed, but it didn't budge. Puzzled, he tried again, with no better luck. Planting his hands on his hips, he regarded the heavy slats of wood that formed the door and spoke over his shoulder. "Is there some trick to this?"

When his question produced no response, he turned. It was hard to see Christine's face in the dim light, but he could feel tension emanating from her, so thick it was almost palpable. He moved toward her, but she pushed past him with such strength he lost his balance. By the time he steadied himself, she was beating on the door with her fists, uttering sounds deep in her throat that reminded him of a wounded animal and sent a chill racing down his spine.

Shocked by her reaction, Dale moved beside her and touched her arm. "Hey, it's okay. Christine, it's okay."

She didn't seem to hear him. She just kept beating on the door, with such force he was afraid she'd hurt herself. Grasping her shoulders, he tried to restrain her, but she flailed at him with surprising strength, writhing in his grasp. Her harsh, erratic breathing was magnified in the confines of the small space, and when a sudden flash of lightning sent a slash of light through the tiny window, he saw the wild look in her eyes. She was terrified, he realized with a jolt.

A loud boom of thunder reverberated in the darkness, and she tried again to jerk free. Dale tightened his grip, convinced that she'd hurt herself—or both of them— if he released her. Belatedly, his professional training kicked in. He knew how to deal with panicked people, had been through Crisis Intervention Team training. He could handle this. He'd just been caught off guard by her extreme—and unexpected—reaction.

"Christine, I'm going to find a way to open the door, okay? Everything will be all right. Christine, I need you to look at me. Come on, look at me."

His voice was calm but commanding. He kept repeating his instructions until her glazed eyes at last focused on his face. "Good. Now listen to me. I'm going to find a way to open the door." His speech was slow and deliberate. "Can you tell me how it locks? Is there something on the outside that keeps the door closed?"

She didn't seem to comprehend the question, and he could feel her shaking beneath his hands, bone-rattling tremors that convulsed her entire body. All at once, her legs buckled, and he tightened his grip to keep her from falling. Easing her down to the floor, he propped her against the wall of the shed. She dropped her head, struggling to draw in ragged, shallow gulps of air, her shoulders heaving.

At this rate it wouldn't be long before she hyperventilated, Dale concluded. He had to get them out of there. Fast. He could try kicking the door down, but given the sturdy boards he suspected the only thing he'd break would be a leg or an ankle.

He dropped to the balls of his feet in front of her and cupped her face in his hands, tilting her head up so she had to look at him. "Okay, Christine. I need you to focus on me. Can you do that? Come on, stay with me. Tell me how the door locks. You can do this. Tell me how the door locks."

A strangled sob caught in her throat, but she managed to choke out a few words. "L-latch. S-swings down."

It wasn't much, but Dale had a pretty good idea what she was talking about. He'd seen a number of outbuildings in the rural area with simple wooden or iron bolts on the doors that swung down to latch behind a U-shaped hook on the frame. He hoped that's what she meant. And he also hoped the door wasn't a tight fit. At least the age of the outbuilding was in his favor on that score. The weathered wood had had plenty of time to shrink.

He removed his hands, and once more Christine's head dropped forward. She pulled her knees up and rested her forehead on them, wrapping her arms around her legs as she huddled into a small, tight ball. She was still shaking violently, but the fight seemed to have gone out of her. Dale had a sudden urge to wrap his arms around her, to hold her until she felt safe, but he suspected that the best way to ease her fear was by setting her free.

Rising, he moved back to the door and peered at the crack where it met the frame. Thanks to the storm, the sky was dark as night, so there was no light to shine through and illuminate any ill-fitting areas. Rather than waste time trying to do a visual check, Dale turned to Christine's tool bench, casting a quick look in her direction. She was only a dim outline in the murky shadows of the shed, but he could tell she hadn't moved a fraction.

A quick scan of the tool bench yielded no useful items. He needed something thin and strong, but few garden implements fit that description. He was beginning to lose hope when several flat metal T-stakes caught his eye, the kind used to identify plants. He'd noticed them in Christine's garden, all neatly labeled. Relief surged through him. One of these might work.

Praying the metal would be thin enough to squeeze between the door and the frame but strong enough to lift the latch, Dale went to work.

It didn't take long. In less than a minute he'd fitted the stake into the crack, located the latch and eased it up. As the door gave way, he pushed it open. Fresh air spilled into the room, along with a faceful of rain as a gust of wind swept toward the opening.

As Dale lifted an arm to wipe the moisture from his eyes with his sleeve, he felt Christine scuttle past on her hands and knees. Caught off balance as she brushed against him, he steadied himself on the door frame, watching as she crawled out onto the gravel path. In seconds the driving rain had soaked through her cotton shirt, plastering it to her slender frame.

Another flash of lightning galvanized Dale into action. Rising, he strode out and pulled her to her feet, urging her toward the house. For once, she didn't fight him. Most likely because her legs weren't yet steady enough to support her weight.

When they reached the shelter of the back porch, he kept one arm around her while he twisted the doorknob. Stepping inside, he flipped on the light to reveal a sunny yellow room with large windows and a skylight that wasn't visible from the front. White cabinets brightened the cheery space, and a large bouquet of flowers stood in the center of an oak table.

He guided Christine in that direction and eased her into a chair. Angling another chair beside her, he sat and scrutinized her face.

The wild terror had subsided, he noted with relief. Her shaking had eased, though occasional tremors continued to ripple through her. No color remained in her cheeks, and there was an unnatural tightness around her eyes. He wouldn't yet call her respiration normal, but he didn't think hyperventilation was an issue any longer.

Satisfied that she wasn't going to pass out, he rose and filled a glass with water. "Try to take a few sips." He passed it to her, guiding her shaking hand with his as she raised it to her lips and swallowed. The day had grown much cooler, and considering that she was soaked, he wasn't surprised when a shiver rippled through her. "You need to get out of those wet clothes."

She drew a shuddering breath and pushed back her damp hair. "You're wet, too." Her voice was raspy, as if she'd overtaxed her vocal chords.

Glancing down, he realized she was right. His slacks were damp, and his shirt was sticking to his back. He flexed his shoulders, but the fabric didn't release its hold. Putting his own discomfort aside, he focused on Christine. "I'll dry. You change while I make some tea."

"Coffee."

"Ah. A woman after my own heart." A brief grin teased his lips.

Rising, Christine took a second to steady herself on the edge of the table, aware that Dale's perceptive eyes missed nothing. Calling on every ounce of her stamina, she pushed away and walked toward the hall, hoping she'd make it to her room without falling flat on her face.

Once there, she could regroup. Assess the damage. Figure out how to deal with the questions she suspected he was saving up until she returned. Questions she wasn't about to answer. She'd already revealed far too much today, including a weakness that could be exploited.

And that scared her.

In the wrong hands, her phobia could become a weapon. It had happened once. She didn't intend for it to happen again.

Her goal was clear. Convince the sheriff that her little performance in the toolshed meant nothing. Explain it in such a way that he'd write it off as a fluke and forget about it.

The only trouble was, she had no idea how to do that. And she also suspected that Dale Lewis had a long memory.

Chapter Seven

As Christine changed into dry clothes, the dull pounding in her head that had begun in the shed intensified. Rummaging through the medicine cabinet in the bathroom, she dug out four aspirin from an unopened bottle. Since coming to Oak Hill, she'd had no need of them. But she'd been prepared. Without aspirin, these headaches escalated to migrainelike pain, almost debilitating in their intensity, leaving her weak and vulnerable. Two things she didn't want to be when she was around the Oak Hill sheriff.

By the time she'd dressed and returned to the kitchen, Dale had made himself at home. Judging by the jacket he now wore—obviously retrieved from his car—and the hum of her dryer, she deduced that he'd ditched his wet shirt. He'd also run a comb through his damp hair. Seated at her kitchen table, he was sipping a mug of coffee. Once more she was subjected to an assessing perusal.

"Feeling better?"

"Yes."

"Your coffee's ready." He nodded toward a steaming mug beside him. "I didn't know how you liked it."

Instead of answering, she retrieved a carton of half-and-half from the fridge and stirred in a generous amount. Once she replaced the cream, she wrapped her hands around the mug and took a sip, hovering behind her chair.

"You can sit, Christine. I won't bite."

His voice was calm, his expression benign. But his probing eyes unnerved her.

Slipping into her seat, she sloshed some coffee on the polished surface. She started to rise again, but he rested a hand on her stiff shoulder.

"Sit."

He moved to the counter and tugged a paper towel from the holder, sopping up the brown liquid and disposing of the soggy mess before retaking his seat. Christine tried to control the tremors in her hands, but as she lifted the mug to her lips they were hard to disguise.

"It looks to me like you could use something stronger than coffee."

At the sheriff's quiet comment, she took a deep breath. He was giving her an opening to talk about the incident. But she chose to turn it into a joke, forcing her uncooperative lips into a slight upward curve as she responded. "Too bad I don't drink."

"You don't have any alcohol in the house?"

The touch of skepticism in his voice puzzled her. "No. Liquor has never held any appeal for me."

A flicker of surprise darted across his face, come and gone so fast she wondered if she'd imagined it. "The coffee will have to do, then. Did you take something for the headache?"

"How do you know I have one?" The man was way too insightful for his own good. Or for her peace of mind.

"Your eyes. They look strained at the corners."

"I thought you were a sheriff, not a doctor."

"I picked up a lot working accidents in L.A. with EMTs. Did you take something?"

He was nothing if not persistent. But there was no harm answering that question, Christine decided. "Yes."

"Have you always had a problem with claustrophobia?"

Nor did he dance around an issue, she concluded, debating how to respond. Jack had asked her that question once, and she'd paid a high price for her admission. Yet in light of what the sheriff had witnessed, her strategy of passing the incident off as a fluke no longer seemed viable. But she could try to play it down.

"Some. It's not a big deal."

"It was a big deal twenty minutes ago, after that door slammed shut." His tone was steady, his gaze intent.

"I would have found a way out eventually." She took a sip of coffee as she framed her response, struggling to swallow past the lump in her throat. "I was just…spooked. And then there was all that thunder and lightning. It was an odd combination of circumstances. I doubt it will ever happen again."

"A lot of people have phobias, Christine. There's nothing wrong with acknowledging that. I'm not all that fond of heights. Do you know how it started?"

"Yes." The cause was etched forever in her memory. "When I was ten, a friend and I found a small cave and decided to explore. I got wedged into a narrow opening, and my friend had to go for help. I wasn't there long, but it was pitch-dark and I couldn't move. I was afraid I was going to suffocate. It was pretty scary for a little kid."

"That would be scary at any age. Do you have this kind of reaction very often?"

"No." *Not anymore.* Wrapping her hands around the mug, she let the warmth seep into her cold fingers.

"What about elevators?"

She avoided them like the plague. If she did find herself in one, she managed to control her fear, but she was always the first to exit the instant the doors slid open.

"I don't freak out, if that's what you're asking. What brought you out here today, anyway?" She hoped Dale would respect the "back off" message implied by her abrupt change of subject.

To her relief, he did.

"I ran into the editor of the *Gazette* and got drafted for courier duty. Your story's in the next issue. Those are some advance copies." He motioned to a stack of newspapers on the counter. "Go ahead and take a look while I finish my coffee. It's a nice article."

"You've read it?"

"Skimmed it when I stopped at the *Gazette* offices to pick up the copies. Page six."

Rising, Christine moved to the counter and flipped through to the correct page. The story occupied the top half of the page and featured two photos, one of her in the garden and a close-up of a bundle of herbs tagged with the Fresh Start Farm label she'd designed. She gave the story a fast read, pleased with the result. It was accurate, complimentary—and good for business.

"That should generate some interest in your weekend pumpkin patch," Dale commented, as if reading her mind.

"There are only two weekends left in October. And I've already sold a lot of the pumpkins that survived."

"How are things working out with Stephen?"

"Better than I expected." Summoning up her courage, she laid the paper on the counter and turned to him. They'd never spoken about the incident since the day he'd stopped by and encouraged her to file an official complaint, but she still resented his interference, even if things had turned out fine. "Why did you talk to Les Mueller?"

"Because you wouldn't." He returned her gaze steadily. "You deserved to be compensated for the damage, and I knew Les would want to make things right."

"I preferred not to make an issue of it."

"You didn't. I did. That's my job, Christine. To see that justice is done."

Cynicism flared in her eyes. She started to respond, but the drier signaled the end of its cycle with a loud, prolonged beep and she clamped her mouth shut. Once quiet again descended, she angled away from him. "Your shirt's dry. Thanks for bringing the papers."

Rising, Dale studied her rigid back. He was being dismissed. She wanted him gone. For some reason, he—and his deputy, according to Marv—made her nervous. In fact, lots of things made her nervous. Small, enclosed spaces. Reporting legitimate misdemeanors. Questions about her past.

The latter was apparent even from his brief scan of the *Gazette* article. She'd been happy to talk about her plans for Fresh Start Farm, her interest in organic farming, her library work. She'd referenced her mother in a couple of quotes, her childhood, her summer job at a nursery in Omaha during high school.

But the article had contained no mention of her married years in Dunlap. Meaning that period in her life must hold the key to her mystery, Dale reasoned. But considering the way she'd shut down, he wasn't going to solve the puzzle today.

Two minutes later, his shirt back on and his jacket dangling by one finger over his shoulder, Dale re-entered the kitchen. Christine remained by the counter, facing him with her hands braced behind her, looking like a cornered animal poised to lunge at the slightest hint of attack.

"I wish I knew why I make you nervous." Dale hadn't planned to open that can of worms, and he immediately regretted speaking. But the words had spilled out before he could contain them.

For a second she seemed taken aback by his quiet comment. He thought she was going to deny it, but instead her tense shoulders sagged, as if the effort of constant vigilance had finally grown too burdensome.

"Look, you seem like a nice man, Sheriff." Her voice was soft, her eyes sad. "I'm sorry if I've offended you. It's nothing personal. I just think it's wise if we keep our distance."

"Why?"

"It's a very long story." She drew an unsteady breath and wrapped her arms around herself, a posture of self-protection that tugged at his heart.

"I don't have to be anywhere for an hour."

Her lips tipped up into a mirthless smile. "That wouldn't even cover chapter one. Let it go."

At some intuitive level, Dale knew that no matter what he said next, Christine wasn't going to budge today. So he did as she asked, murmuring a quick goodbye and heading back to the patrol car.

But as he pulled down the drive and passed the Fresh Start Farm sign, his jaw settled into a determined line. Sooner or later he was going to uncover the real meaning behind the name of Christine's new enterprise.

And he preferred that it be sooner.

Two nights later, a persistent thumping tugged Christine out of a deep sleep. Groggy, she blinked and tried to identify the sound. Knocking. That was it. Someone was knocking on her front door. At…she propped herself up on one elbow and peered at her bedside clock. Eleven o'clock. Late for a farmer. And definitely too late for callers.

When the frantic pounding started up again, a surge of adrenaline shot through her. Swinging her feet to the floor, she shrugged into her robe and crept down the stairs from her second-floor bedroom, cell phone in hand. She had good locks. Installing them had been her first order of business after she'd moved in. But she wasn't taking any chances.

Her fingers poised to dial 9-1-1, she tiptoed to the peephole in the door and glanced through.

The tableau on the other side was like a punch in the stomach.

Erin and Brian stood on the doorstep, illuminated by the dusk-to-dawn lantern beside the door. Though their images were distorted by the fishbowl lens, Erin's black eye and bleeding, split lip were impossible to miss.

Her hands shaking, Christine fumbled with the lock. When she opened the door, Erin surged forward, almost falling into her arms. Christine pulled her inside, noting that Brian's face was pasty and that he had a death grip on his mother's hand. His eyes were wide with fear as he darted a look at Christine.

"I'm so sorry to bother you this late. But you offered to help, and I—I didn't know where else to go." A sob choked Erin's voice as Christine guided her into the living room and eased her onto the couch.

"It's no bother, Erin." Christine sat beside her and took her hand. She didn't have to be told the source of Erin's injuries, and the woman seemed to know that. "Have you called the sheriff?"

"No. That will make things worse."

Christine understood Erin's position. Better than her visitor would ever know. And a few months ago, she'd have agreed with her.

But that was before she'd met Dale Lewis. Never again had she expected to be able to put one iota of trust in a cop. Yet the Oak Hill sheriff had slowly begun to convince her that he was what he seemed— a man dedicated to seeing that justice was done. A man of integrity and honor, who could be counted on to uphold the law. A man who would ease Erin's burden, not add to it.

Transferring her attention to Brian, she looked him over. Other than being scared, he appeared to be untouched. But she needed to be sure. "Is Brian okay?"

"Yes."

Physically, perhaps. But his lower lip had begun to quiver, and his freckles stood out in stark relief against his pale skin.

"My daddy hurt my mommy."

His tearful statement clutched at Christine's heart. "We're going to fix her all up, though. She's going to be fine." Looking back at Erin, she saw the anxiety in the woman's eyes.

"I took the car." Erin's words were riddled with fear. "Derrick went out drinking with some buddies after…" She swallowed and left the sentence unfinished. "But he'll be home soon, and he'll come looking for me. I shouldn't have panicked. He'll be furious when he finds out I left. I have to go back."

"Erin, you can't do that. It's not safe—for either of you."

"I don't have anywhere else to go. And I don't have any money. Everything's in Derrick's name."

There were questions Christine needed to ask, but not in front of Brian. She looked at him again. Despite the strain of the evening, the little boy's eyelids were growing heavy. Christine seized that opportunity.

"Have you ever slept on a window seat, Brian?"

"What's a window seat?" The boy gave her a puzzled look.

She pointed to the bay window along one wall of the living room. A bench topped with thick cushions lined the inside. "I like to sit there and read. And it's a great spot for a nap. Would you like to try it?"

It was just across the room, close enough that Brian could hear the murmur of their voices but far enough away that he'd be unable to distinguish their words if they spoke softly.

"That's a good idea, honey." Erin caught Christine's drift and managed to smile at the little boy. "Mommy will be right here."

Without waiting for him to reply, Christine rose and snagged an afghan off a nearby chair and a cushion from the corner of the couch. "We missed you at story hour yesterday, Brian." She spoke in a normal, conversational tone as she took his hand. "I had some oatmeal cookies left, and I saved some for you. Tomorrow you can try them." As she talked, she led him over to the window seat and helped him climb up.

"I like oatmeal cookies." He yawned and snuggled under the afghan.

"I thought you might." She brushed his fine hair back from his forehead. As bad as her situation had been, at least no children had been involved. Although her two miscarriages had been traumatic, her sorrow had given way almost to relief over time. No child deserved to grow up in an atmosphere of fear and intimidation.

Including Brian.

Resolution stiffening her shoulders, she returned

to the couch. "You need medical attention, Erin. At least let me call Dr. Martin."

"I'll be okay."

"Are you injured anywhere besides your face?" Once again, the woman was wearing a turtleneck top.

"I think my wrist might be sprained." Erin's gaze flickered to her left hand, lying limp in her lap.

"I'm calling Dr. Martin."

Expecting further protest, Christine was surprised when Erin didn't object. After looking up the doctor's number and placing the call, she rejoined the young mother. "He'll be here in a few minutes. Now let's talk about calling the sheriff."

"No." Fear coursed through Erin's eyes. "He's come to the house a few times, after the neighbors reported a disturbance. Derrick was furious. It was worse after he left."

"It won't be worse if you don't go back."

"I'm afraid not to. He'll find me. And h-he'll hurt Brian. He said if I ever told anyone about this, or tried to leave, he'd track us down and Brian would pay the consequences."

"He threatened his own son?" Christine choked back the disgust that clawed at her throat.

"That's the problem. I had Brian when I was eighteen. I wasn't married, and his father wanted nothing to do with me or the baby. I met Derrick two years ago, and I thought I could trust him. He was older, and he said he loved me and didn't mind that

I already had a son. I was grateful someone wanted us. But we were only married a month when he started using threats to Brian as a way to control me."

Blackmail. There was no more effective weapon than a threat to someone you loved, as Christine knew too well. It could trap you in a nightmare. But unlike Christine, Erin had a way out.

"You can't continue to live in that kind of environment." Christine took the young woman's hand in an urgent grip. "One of these days, your husband is going to hurt you far worse than he already has. Some abused women are killed, Erin. Do you want Brian to grow up with that man if you're not there to protect him?"

What little color remained in Erin's face drained away. Christine hated to add to her stress, but if scare tactics were needed to convince her to take action, she wasn't above using them.

"You have to report this to the sheriff. He'll get a restraining order making it illegal for your husband to bother you. The state will have something to say about your husband's assets. The Legal Aid Society can provide free legal assistance. And you're welcome to stay with me until you get on your feet."

"You'd let me stay here?" Tears pooled in Erin's eyes, and a flicker of hope eased the lines of strain around her mouth.

"If that's what it takes."

With one more glance at her sleeping son, Erin straightened her shoulders. "Okay. I'll talk to the sheriff."

Dale had just dozed off when his pager began to vibrate. Though Oak Hill had few middle-of-the-night emergencies, he always kept the device within reach. His years as a cop in L.A. had taught him that in emergency situations, seconds could mean the difference between life and death.

Swinging his feet to the floor, he picked up the phone and checked in with the 9-1-1 dispatcher. Since joining the staff, Marv had been happy to handle the few late-night calls that had come in, and Dale planned to pass this one on to his deputy, too. Dale didn't mind taking the calls himself, but he hated to disrupt his daughter's sleep and wake his mother by dropping her off. Limited backup was one of the few disadvantages of being a small-town sheriff.

When the dispatcher answered, Dale identified himself. "What's up?"

"Domestic violence incident."

The Carsons, he assumed. But the address the dispatcher rattled off didn't match.

"Who called in the report?"

"A Christine Turner."

Shock rippled through him. Christine did live on the rural route the dispatcher had noted. But the pieces weren't fitting. Rising, Dale juggled the phone as he slid his arms into his shirt. He wasn't passing this one on to Marv, after all. "Has an ambulance been dispatched?"

"No. The caller said it wasn't needed."

"I'm on my way."

Twelve minutes later, after handing a sleepy Jenna into his mother's waiting arms, Dale headed out of town, covering the distance to Christine's farm in record time. There were two cars parked in front of her house. One was unfamiliar. The other belonged to Sam Martin.

His adrenaline pumping, Dale ascended the four steps leading to her front door in two leaps.

Before he could press the bell, Christine pulled the door open. A soft velour robe was cinched at her waist, and her feet were bare. She looked distressed but unhurt, and Dale let out the breath he hadn't realized he was holding.

"Are you all right?"

She nodded and put a finger to her lips as she motioned him in, pointing toward a sleeping Brian Carson.

"We're trying not to wake him. He's had a tough night."

So this was about Erin after all. "What happened?"

She gave him a quick recap, concluding with her call to Dr. Martin. "He's with her in the kitchen."

"And she's willing to file a formal complaint this time?"

"Yes."

"How did you manage that?"

"I convinced her she had to do it for Brian's sake, as well as her own." Christine started toward the back of the house, speaking over her shoulder. "And I offered her a place to stay until she gets on her feet."

A rush of fear surged through Dale, tightening his gut. He grabbed her arm, halting her in midstride as he forced her to face him. "That could be very dangerous."

"Not if you get a restraining order."

"That doesn't stop some guys."

"He doesn't have to know she's here."

"Word will get out."

Resolution lifted her chin. "The offer's been made. I'm not retracting it." She tugged on her arm, but when he didn't relinquish it a trace of the fear he'd seen in her eyes the rainy night they'd met echoed in their depths.

He loosened his grip at once, but he wanted answers. "Why, Christine? Why are you putting yourself in the line of fire?"

"If you do your job, there won't be any fire."

"I can't guard your place night and day."

"I don't expect you to."

"A shelter in Rolla is a better option for her."

"No, it isn't. Erin already feels scared and alone. She needs support. I have room. It's not open for discussion, Sheriff." With that, she pulled her arm free and walked toward the kitchen.

It took Dale a good sixty seconds to temper his frustration and tamp down his fear. Christine Turner was one stubborn woman. And she was taking a very big risk.

While Dale could appreciate her generosity from a Christian perspective, his professional opinion was different. Experience had taught him to be cautious and avoid confrontation unless left with no other option. And there were other options for Erin and her son. Yet Christine refused to consider them. He didn't like that. Not one little bit.

And despite her last comment, he did intend to discuss it with her further.

Chapter Eight

Pushing open the door to the kitchen, Dale took in the scene. Erin was seated at the table, an ice pack pressed to her eye while Sam Martin wrapped her wrist with an elastic bandage. Christine stood beside Erin, a hand on the young woman's shoulder, her expression defiant.

After securing the bandage, Sam stood and looked toward the door. "Hi, Dale. I'm just finishing up." He began to gather up his supplies, and Christine moved from behind Erin to assist him. As she reached for a pack of gauze, Sam let out a low whistle and took her hand. "What on earth did you do to yourself?"

In three long strides, Dale was beside them, eyeing a puffy, purple bruise that ran along the outside of Christine's hand. She tucked her other hand into the deep pocket of her robe, but Dale didn't need to see it to know it bore a matching bruise. Two days ago, as she'd banged on the toolshed door, he'd been afraid she would hurt herself. It was clear he hadn't moved fast enough to save her from injury.

"It's a long and boring story," Christine told Sam, shooting Dale a warning glance. "I'll be fine."

The doctor didn't look convinced. When a gentle prod produced an audible wince, he shook his head. "You might want to have this X-rayed."

"If it doesn't get better in a few days, I'll think about it." She retrieved her hand and tucked it in her other pocket. "Thank you for coming out tonight, Doctor. I'm sorry I had to bother you at such a late hour."

"It wasn't a bother." He looked down at Erin and addressed his next comment to her. "Call me if you have any further problems."

By the time Christine returned from walking Sam to the door, Dale was taking Erin's statement. As she set about brewing a pot of coffee, Christine was impressed with his professional yet considerate approach. He didn't badger, didn't push, didn't make Erin feel like the accused instead of the accuser. He treated her like the victim she was, his demeanor serious, his manner empathetic.

Where had he been when she'd needed a sympathetic cop?

Turning away from the two people seated at the kitchen table, Christine thought back to the night she'd confronted Jack about the rumors of his indiscretions. Though she'd been disappointed that their marriage had never lived up to the expectations created by their romantic, whirlwind courtship, their relationship had degenerated rapidly in the two months after Jack's father died.

While she had already grown accustomed to his extended absences, distraction and late nights at the office, his touchiness and irritability were new. But she'd attributed all of it to grief and to the stress of running the business he'd inherited, and she'd done her best to overlook his unpleasant attitude.

She hadn't been able to overlook the rumors of infidelity she'd overheard in the ladies room at the nursing home while visiting her mother, however. Inside the stall, she'd listened as two aides had discussed her visit. One had commented how faithful she was, and the other had laughed and remarked that it was a shame her husband didn't follow her example. The woman then proceeded to fill in her coworker on his longstanding reputation as a ladies' man, noting that marriage hadn't seemed to change that and passing on the most recent rumor she'd heard.

That night at dinner, as she'd picked at her food while Jack read a magazine, she'd worked up the courage to raise the subject. He hadn't been pleased about being questioned and had tried to brush her off. But after she'd persisted, noting how little time they spent together and asking if he'd stopped loving her, his irritability had soared to fury so fast her head had reeled.

The explosion, when it came, reminded her of a stick of dynamite that had just been waiting for the touch of a match. He'd grabbed her arm and half dragged her down the hall, saying that if she wanted him in her bed she had only to ask.

Shocked by his violent response, she'd fought him, searching without success for some trace of the charming man who had wooed her, terrified by the Jekyll and Hyde transformation. She'd used every ounce of her strength to resist him, but she'd been no match for his well-honed muscles.

She could still remember the sound of cloth ripping as he'd torn at her clothes, could still feel the rough groping of his hands. And as he'd transformed an act of love into punishment, the fading romantic dreams she'd been clinging to evaporated as quickly and completely as a puff of warm breath on a cold, frosty morning.

Throughout that ordeal, as tears had streamed down her cheeks, Christine had begged God to help her. But it seemed He'd been otherwise occupied. Nor had He been around when Jack had tired of that game and turned to another. Too numb at that point to offer much resistance, she'd had no idea what he planned to do as he'd pulled her off the bed, grabbed her wrist and hauled her across the room.

Only when he'd opened the closet door, shoved her inside and slammed it shut had she realized his intent. Although she had questioned him about having the lock installed a few weeks before, she'd accepted his explanation that he didn't trust the cleaning woman.

But then, as the lock clicked, she'd realized he'd been preparing for this day. Readying a prison for her.

Frantic once again, she'd pounded on the door until her hands were bruised and swollen, pleading for release as the first of the many near-debilitating headaches to come pounded in her temples.

An hour later, when he'd at last opened the door, she had been too spent to do more than lie like a limp rag doll in one corner. But she'd remembered the cold, hard edge to his words as he'd glared down at her.

"Let's get something straight, Christine. Now that dad's gone, I do what I want, when I want, with whomever I want. My marriage to a prim and proper little librarian convinced him I was ready to settle down—and to name me his successor in the business. So it accomplished its main purpose.

"However, since this is Bible country, it's advantageous for me to maintain the image of a devoted married man. If you play the part of a loving wife in public, everything will be fine. But stay out of the rest of my life."

It had taken her hours to recover. Hours to process the bombshell he'd dropped about the reason he'd married her. Hours to acknowledge that her romantic fantasies had never been anything more than that. And hours to gather the courage to report the incident to the police, waiting until she heard Jack's car pull out of the driveway before picking up the phone.

Like Oak Hill, Dunlap had a tiny police department, consisting of Sheriff Gary Stratton and two part-time deputies. Gary had responded to the call. She'd known that the cocky, fortysomething lawman and Jack were buddies, but it had never occurred to her that the man would put friendship above the law. Nor that he would be willing to accept "favors" in return for keeping her in line.

A shudder ran through her as Christine recalled that terrible night. By the time Gary had shown up at the door, her hands had already begun to discolor and she'd been limping from a wrenched knee. As she'd related her sordid story, she'd sensed his resistance. More than once he'd interrupted her to ask if she was sure everything she was relating had happened. He'd taken no copious notes, as Dale was now doing with Erin. In fact, he hadn't even pulled out his notebook until she'd questioned him about it, and then he'd written little.

In the middle of her statement, Jack had come home. She would never forget the barely contained rage that had ignited in his eyes when he'd realized she'd called the police. But he'd been good at masking his feelings. And he'd always been a smooth talker. The look he sent her was venomous, but the smile he gave Gary was genial.

"What's going on here, Sheriff?"

"Your wife called. Said you attacked her."

Feigning concern, Jack had moved beside her. She'd flinched and tried to step away, but his hand had tightened around her wrist in an iron grip.

"Have you been at the bourbon again, honey?" His tone was solicitous, his gaze pointed as a lance as he spoke to her. Transferring his attention to Gary, he'd lowered his voice. "We try to keep her little problem on the quiet side, Sheriff. You understand."

Stunned, she'd gaped at him. But shock had quickly given way to rage. Jerking free, she'd faced the man who was sworn to uphold the law. "That's a lie. I don't drink. And he did attack me."

Gary had glanced at Jack, who'd given a "what-can-you-do" shrug. Turning to Christine, the sheriff had cleared his throat. "That's kinda hard to verify, ma'am, you being his wife and all."

"I have the bruises to prove I resisted."

Jack had stepped in at that point, throwing an arm around her rigid shoulders, his fingers digging into her flesh. "She does have a lot of bruises. Liquor can make you pretty unsteady. You know how it is, Sheriff." He'd given the man a conspiratorial wink. "I've taken a few spills myself through the years. I bet you have, too. Not on duty, of course." He'd nudged Gary in the ribs with his elbow, and the two had shared a chuckle. "Why don't you let me walk you out?"

The man had closed his notebook while an incredulous Christine had watched. "Aren't you going to do anything about my complaint?"

"Well, ma'am, why don't we see how it goes?" His tone had been placating and condescending. "Maybe you'll feel different about things tomorrow."

"That's the spirit." Jack had slapped the sheriff on the back. "Give her a chance to sleep it off. Let me walk you out, Sheriff."

While Christine had looked on, the two men had ambled out to Gary's patrol car. They'd both laughed over some remark Jack had made. Then her husband had extracted his wallet and discreetly handed over a few bills, which the man had pocketed. Jack had waved the sheriff off with a smile, but as he'd swung toward the house, all levity had vanished from his countenance.

That's when her life had become a living nightmare.

Because much as she'd wanted to walk out, he'd played a card she couldn't trump.

A hand on her shoulder jolted her back to reality, and Christine jerked.

"Sorry. I didn't mean to startle you. I think Erin could use a cup of that coffee." Dale's assessing gaze missed nothing, and the twin furrows in his brow deepened. "It looks like you could, too." She started to reach for two mugs, but Dale stilled her with a gentle touch on her arm and dropped his volume. "If you're having second thoughts, I can contact the shelter in Rolla."

"No." In the past twenty-four months, Christine had had second thoughts about many things. But not about this decision. "Erin and Brian are going to stay here."

And there was nothing the sheriff could say or do that would change her mind.

* * *

There was a strange car parked in her driveway.

As Christine turned in at the Fresh Start Farm sign, she eased back on the gas pedal, apprehension nipping at her composure. She'd told Dale last night that she wasn't afraid to have Erin stay with her, but in truth it unnerved her. She knew how unpredictable sadistic, violent people could be. Erin's husband was apt to do anything if he discovered where his wife was.

But Dale had taken pains to keep her location a secret. He'd moved his patrol car to the rear of Christine's house the night before and driven Erin's car home. First thing that morning, Marv had dropped him off so he could pick up the patrol car. Restraining order in hand, he'd called on Derrick and handed both it and the car over to him. At least that was the message Erin had relayed when Christine had checked in with her around midmorning from the farmers' market.

After last night's excitement, Christine would like nothing better than to curl up in her bed and take a good, long nap. But she had a feeling that wasn't likely to happen. Not if she had yet another visitor.

Nothing seemed amiss as she drew close, but she stopped a safe distance away, knowing the quiet could be deceptive. Pulling out her cell phone, she started to dial the house number. A quick conversation with Erin might be prudent before she went in. But her concern dissipated when a grinning Brian pushed through the front door and waved at her.

"Hi, Ms. Christine." He bounded down the steps as she slid from the cab of her truck.

"Hello, Brian. Looks like we have company."

"Yeah. It's Reverend Andrews. Mom called him."

As she'd helped Erin unpack the meager belongings the young mother had thrown into a suitcase before bolting from her house, Christine had noticed a Bible. Considering the bad experiences Erin had already endured in her young life, she'd been surprised to discover that the woman was religious. But if she found comfort in reading the Bible and visiting with her minister, Christine didn't begrudge her either. In light of her own lapsed faith, however, she wasn't anxious to rub elbows with a man of the cloth.

When Christine held back, Brian took her hand and tugged her toward the house. "Don't worry. He's nice. Besides, Mom wouldn't let me eat those oatmeal cookies until you got home. So can you tell her it's okay?"

Since refusing to enter her own house seemed childish, Christine let Brian lead her inside. She would say a quick hello, give Brian his cookies, then hang out in the kitchen until the man left.

"Hey, Mom, Ms. Christine is home," he called as they came through the door.

With Brian still tugging on her hand, Christine followed him to the living room. Erin was seated beside a sandy-haired, fortyish man who smiled and rose as she entered.

Casting a nervous glance her way, Erin spoke. "I hope you don't mind, Christine, but I asked Reverend Andrews to stop by."

"No problem."

"I've heard many good things about you from a lot of people in my congregation." The man took a step forward and held out his hand. "I'm Craig Andrews."

Wiping her damp palm on her jeans, Christine returned the handshake, disarmed despite herself by the sincerity and warmth in his eyes. "Christine Turner."

"We're almost finished," Erin told her.

"Take your time. Brian and I are going to check out those oatmeal cookies, aren't we, Brian?"

"Yeah!"

"Nice to meet you, Reverend." With that, Christine escaped to the kitchen.

Fifteen minutes later, as Brian finished his cookies and headed out to "help" Stephen, who had just arrived, a discreet tap sounded on the door that led from the hall to the kitchen.

"Ms. Turner? May I come in?"

It was the minister. She had no desire to talk to him, but short of following Brian's example and disappearing out the back door, there was no way around it. "Yes, of course."

As he pushed open the door, she rose. "Can I get you some coffee?"

"No, thank you. I need to be on my way. But I couldn't leave without thanking you for what you're doing for Erin."

"It's not a big deal." Dismissing his comment with a shrug, Christine braced her hands on the back of the chair, putting it between the two of them.

"On the contrary. I think it's a great example of Christian charity in action."

"Believe me, I didn't do it for that reason."

"I didn't mean to offend you." Her sharp response brought a quizzical lift to his eyebrows. "I take it you're not a Christian?"

"The Lord and I parted ways some time ago."

"I'm sorry to hear that."

To her surprise, there was no recrimination in his inflection, no judgment. Just genuine sorrow. Thrown by his response, she shrugged again and lifted her chin. "I'm fine, Reverend. I have no need of a God who doesn't care about His people."

A speculative expression flitted across his face, and she thought he was going to pursue the discussion. But he took a different tack. "If charity wasn't the motivation for your kindness, may I ask what was?"

His tone was relaxed and undemanding, but his eyes were alert. Dale Lewis wasn't the only astute man in this town, she concluded. And she couldn't fault the minister's diligence. After all, it was his job to bring in lost sheep. Except this sheep didn't want bringing in.

"I'm afraid it's a very long story." She gave him a half smile. "Are you sure I can't interest you in coffee?"

To his credit, he didn't push. "No, thank you. Erin is…"

As he uttered her name, she came through the door. There was a brightness in her eyes, a hope, that Christine had never seen before.

"Our prayer was answered, Reverend. The Lord softened his heart. He said I could come."

Confused, Christine looked from one to the other.

"Erin has a stepbrother on the East Coast. She hasn't seen him in almost five years, and their parting was less than friendly."

"When I got pregnant, he was very angry. He said I'd sinned, and that he didn't want anything more to do with me." A soft flush rose on Erin's cheeks. "I moved to St. Louis and stayed with a friend until I got a job and an apartment. That's where I met Derrick. I wrote Bill after I got married, but he never responded. He's married now himself, and has a little girl. He said he was sorry we'd had a falling out, and that I could stay with him until I got settled. He's even wiring me the money for the bus fare."

"This is a wonderful opportunity, Erin." The minister placed a hand on her shoulder. "A chance for a fresh start. Like the name of the farm that gave you refuge. An interesting designation, by the way." The latter comment was directed to Christine.

She ignored his remark, focusing instead on Erin.

"You should let the sheriff know. He'll need to fill you in on any legalities involved before you leave the state."

"I'll call him right away." She held out her hand to the minister. "Thank you again, Reverend. Please keep me in your prayers."

"Always." He cocooned her hand between his. "God go with you, Erin."

With a smile, she retreated to the living room. A few seconds later they heard her footsteps on the stairs.

The minister withdrew a card from his pocket and laid it on the table. "If you ever want to share that long story, I've been told I'm a good listener. In the meantime, think about joining us some Sunday for services. No obligation. The singing is quite rousing, and we have a lively social hour afterward." He flashed her an affable grin.

It was hard not to like the man. And impossible to question his sincerity. Christine might be wary of men in general, and sheriffs in particular, but she had nothing against clerics. If ever she did need a sympathetic ear, Craig Andrews might be the person to call.

"Thank you. I'll keep that in mind."

"Please do. And may I leave you with one thought? Whatever your reason for turning away from God, remember that He's never turned away from you. He's always there, even in the darkness when we can't see Him clearly. All we have to do is open our hearts and invite Him in."

Her throat constricted, and her response came out choked. "It's been my experience that He doesn't always hear that invitation."

"He always hears, Christine." The minister's words were gentle. "But His timetable doesn't always match ours. And His ways are sometimes difficult to understand. Accepting without understanding is one of the great challenges of our faith."

"Not everyone is up to that challenge."

"I have a feeling I'm looking at someone who is."

"You give me too much credit."

A smile touched his lips. "No more than God does." With a firm, encouraging handshake, he was gone.

Long after the minister left, Christine remained in the kitchen. Erin's Bible sat on the table, and Christine picked it up. Once, she'd consulted it often for solace and hope. But in the end, the austere black words on the white paper had seemed as cold and empty as a betrayed heart.

Now, she flipped through the pages, letting the book fall open wherever it chose. It was a game she used to play, picking a quote at random and applying it to her life. Today the book opened to Hebrews. And she didn't have to select a verse; one jumped out at her. "Let us therefore draw near with confidence to the throne of grace, that we may obtain mercy and find grace to help in time of need."

She knew the verse well. It had been one of her favorites, and as things had become unbearable with

Jack, she'd clung to it, believing that eventually God would hear her plea for help.

According to the minister, He *had* heard her. But when her prayers hadn't been answered in the way she'd wanted, with immediate release from her tormentor, she'd assumed He wasn't listening and had turned away from Him.

Yet all at once she wondered if perhaps God had given her help of a different kind: the grace to endure. In retrospect, she doubted whether she could have survived without assistance from a greater power. As for why He'd wanted her to endure—that was less clear. But as Reverend Andrews had pointed out, it wasn't always possible to comprehend God's ways. The challenge was to accept without understanding.

She wasn't at that point yet. Not even close. But for the first time since she'd shut God out of her life, she wondered if perhaps He'd stayed by her side all along, just out of sight, in the shadows that had darkened her world. When she'd felt most alone and abandoned, had He been near, waiting for her to reach out and claim the comfort He offered? Had she given up on prayer too soon?

The answers to those questions eluded her. But as she fingered the minister's card, she knew she had to search for them. And she also knew where to start.

Chapter Nine

Reverend Andrews had been right. The music was rousing.

For the first time since she'd edged into a vacant seat in the last row of the church, moments after the service began, Christine relaxed. During the past week, as October wound to a close and she'd finished out the season at the farmers' markets, her initial resolution to attend services had wavered. But a conversation with Erin and Brian two days ago, as she saw them off at the bus station in Rolla, had given her the push she needed.

She'd hugged the young woman, then stooped to do the same with Brian, gathering the youngster in her arms before handing him a sack of oatmeal cookies. "In case you get hungry along the way," she'd told him.

A lopsided grin had been her reward, followed by a troubled expression. "I wish I had a present for you.

Mom says that because of you, everything will be better from now on."

"My best present is seeing you both happy and all ready to start a brand-new life," Christine had reassured him with a smile, ruffling his hair.

Unappeased, he'd wrinkled his nose and squinted in concentration. Than all at once his features had relaxed. "I know! I'll pray for you! Maybe God will give you a present for me, if I ask Him." He'd looked up at Erin. "Is that a good idea, Mom?"

"That's a great idea, honey. God always listens to our prayers."

"That's very nice, Brian." Christine had forced her lips into a smile. "Thank you."

When she'd stood, Erin had touched her arm. "I couldn't have done this without your support, Christine. I don't have a gift, either, but I think Brian came up with the best idea. I'll pray for you, too."

Feeling awkward, Christine had shoved her hands into the pockets of her jacket. "Use your prayers for yourself, Erin. You still have a long road ahead."

"God's led me this far. I know He'll be with me whatever happens. He's with you, too."

The absolute trust and confidence on the young mother's face as she'd echoed Reverend Andrews's words had evoked a twinge of envy in Christine.

Brian had tugged on Erin's sleeve. "The people are getting on the bus, Mom."

"You'll let me know how you're doing?" Christine had given her one last hug.

"Of course. Once we're settled, I'll write or call. Besides, I'll need to stay in touch to see if my prayers for you are being answered."

"What exactly are you praying for?" Christine had given her a curious look.

"Healing. And homecoming."

Erin's insight had shocked Christine. The two women had never talked of Christine's past, nor her estrangement from God. But in Christine, the young, battered wife must have sensed a kindred spirit. And a lost soul.

As Christine had watched the two of them climb the steps to the bus—a woman whose faith and hope had endured despite her tribulations, and a little boy clutching a bag of oatmeal cookies who continued to believe in a better tomorrow despite the trauma that had plagued his young life—she'd resolved to try and find her way out of the spiritual wilderness in which she'd been wandering. After all, if even a child was praying for her, how could she do anything less?

So here she sat, wedged into the last space at the back of church, feeling a bit like a fraud. If the heartfelt rendition of the songs was any indication, this was a solid, spirit-filled faith community. Doubters didn't belong. Yet Reverend Andrews had encouraged her to attend, despite her outspoken comments about the Lord. Perhaps he'd thought her attitude might soften if she found herself surrounded by believers.

If that was his hope, to some degree it was being realized, she acknowledged. Participating in Sunday services had always bolstered her faith. That old saying about strength in numbers must apply to religion as well. And she needn't have worried that anyone would sense her misgivings and send disapproving looks her way. She'd been the recipient of nothing but friendly, welcoming smiles.

In the end, Christine found the experience worthwhile. It didn't dispel all her doubts, nor did she feel she'd reestablished the personal relationship with the Lord that she'd once enjoyed. But Reverend Andrews's sermon on the prodigal son—an odd coincidence, she reflected—was thought-provoking, and the familiar prayers heartwarming. Considering that she'd expected to be turned off, it wasn't a bad start. She might even come back.

As the service ended, Christine rose, planning to make a fast exit. But when she pushed through the door at the back of church, the final notes of the last hymn fading behind her, she found Marge waiting. How in the world had the innkeeper beat her out? And why hadn't she spotted the woman's hot-pink blazer in church? It seemed to glow.

"I recognized your truck in the parking lot." Marge met her at the bottom of the steps and pumped her hand. "Welcome. I'm glad you decided to join us.

The social hour is in the church hall, downstairs. I came to the earlier service, but I help set up and serve for the social hour after this one."

That explained why Christine hadn't noticed her in church.

"I wasn't planning to stay, Marge. I had a busy week, and I've got some catching up to do at home. Maybe one of these…"

"Christine? I thought that was you." Cara Martin came up, followed by Sam. "I was just telling Marge that I'm going to be lost without your fresh herbs once the cooler weather really sets in. You've spoiled me. And when are you going to stop by the inn for dinner? The first one's on the house, remember. You're staying for coffee today, aren't you?"

"I'm afraid I have a whole list of chores at home, and…"

"Christine! I'm so glad you stopped by." Reverend Andrews joined the growing group, taking Christine's hand in a warm clasp.

"We're trying to convince her to stay for the social hour," Marge told him.

"Of course you'll stay. Marge makes excellent coffee. And we have chocolate donuts today. My personal favorite."

"I appreciate the invitation, but…"

"Ms. Christine!"

The group turned en masse as Jenna's excited voice carried over the crowd congregating at the base of the steps below the church door. Arlene held her hand on one side, Dale on the other as they prepared to descend. But it was a Dale Christine had never seen before.

Gone was the intimidating official uniform. In its place was a dark gray suit that emphasized his broad shoulders. A maroon and midnight-blue tie lay against a snowy white shirt, and gold cuff links gleamed at his wrists. He looked…fabulous. And very, very appealing. For the first time in their acquaintance, she noticed the man instead of the badge.

If Christine was stunned, Dale was no less surprised. The last person he'd expected to see in church was the antisocial organic farmer, who went out of her way to avoid mingling with the locals.

And she looked…different today. Instead of her customary jeans and work shirts, she wore a sleek black skirt that showed off enough leg to send his blood pressure up a few notches. A wide belt nipped in a supple silk blouse at her small waist, and her hair lay soft and loose against her shoulders, the red highlights sparking in the sun. The flat gold necklace that dipped just below the round neckline of her blouse glittered in the morning light with each breath she drew.

As for his own breath—she'd taken it away. He'd told Jenna once that the mystery lady was pretty, but he'd lied. She was flat-out gorgeous.

"Dale?"

His mother interrupted his appreciative perusal, and he dragged his attention away from Christine.

"It's not polite to stare." The twinkle in her eyes took the criticism out of her words. "And we're holding up the crowd."

A hot flush crept up the back of his neck and he continued down the steps without a word.

"Daddy, aren't we going to say hi to Ms. Christine?" Jenna inquired when he headed toward the entrance to the church hall.

"Of course we are. It wouldn't be polite not to." Arlene took Jenna's hand in a firmer grip and switched directions.

Dale found himself being pulled along.

"It's nice to see you, Christine," Arlene greeted her with a warm smile. "I was telling Dale this morning how much we enjoy story hour. You've made it so much fun, I don't know who looks forward to it more—me or Jenna."

Trying to ignore the tall man holding Jenna's other hand, Christine focused on his mother. Except for Dale's one visit, Arlene always brought Jenna to the library for the weekly story hour. And she never left without saying a few pleasant words to Christine. Her own mother would have liked Arlene, Christine reflected. The women shared a natural empathy and sincerity that drew people in. If Arlene wasn't the sheriff's mother, Christine would have enjoyed getting to know her better.

"I understand it's quite a hit," Marge chimed in.

"Maybe I should come and check it out," Cara remarked, reaching for Sam's hand. There was an undercurrent of excitement in her voice. "One never knows when one will need a story hour."

A few beats of silence ticked by as a slow smile tugged at Marge's lips. "Does this mean what I think it does?"

As Sam drew Cara close, tucking her beside him, she grinned. "Yep. We just found out for sure. In seven months, give or take a week or two, Oak Hill will have a brand-new citizen."

"Now isn't this grand news!" Marge engulfed Cara in a bear hug as congratulations sounded all around. Christine added her own best wishes, quickly stepping back as a wistful melancholy tightened her throat. Her own dreams of motherhood had been as elusive as the wood sprites who peopled some of the books she read to the children.

She blinked back the sudden moisture that clouded her vision, but not fast enough. Dale, too, stood a bit apart from the group clustered around Cara, one hand in the pocket of his slacks, and he was watching her. His blue eyes deepened in color, delving, as if he was trying to get a handle on the woman he'd termed "the mystery lady."

Anxious to escape his intent gaze, Christine dropped down to Jenna's level and smiled at the little girl. "You look very pretty today, Jenna."

"Thank you." The compliment brought a sunny smile to her lips. Then she edged closer and gave Christine a puzzled look. "Why is everybody so happy?"

"Because Dr. Martin's wife is going to have a baby."

"I like babies." Her face lit up. "Do you think she might let me hold it?"

"I think she might."

"Do you like babies, Ms. Christine?"

What was that old saying about jumping from the frying pan into the fire? She'd leapt in feetfirst. "Yes."

"Have you ever had a baby, Ms. Christine?"

"No, honey." The answer came out in a hoarse whisper.

"Would you like to have one?"

"Jenna, it's time to go in for donuts." Dale moved beside his daughter, resting his hands on her shoulders.

He had nice hands, Christine reflected, afraid to lift her head in case her eyes reflected the desolation in her heart. Instead, she studied the lean, strong fingers that looked competent for any task he might undertake. Holding his own against an attacking lawbreaker. Opening a locked toolshed door. Tucking in a little girl. Caressing a woman.

Jolted by that unbidden thought, Christine felt warm color steal over cheeks. Where had that come from? She didn't have any interest in Dale Lewis in that way. Nor in any man. Been there, done that. She wasn't about to risk repeating her mistake.

But she was curious about him. Since he wore no

ring, she assumed he hadn't remarried. And what had happened to his wife? Had Christine mingled with the locals a bit more, she'd have found out his story by now, she was sure. Being out of the loop was one of the downsides to her chosen lifestyle.

"Are you coming for donuts, too, Ms. Christine?" Jenna inquired.

Standing, Christine started to shake her head as Marge answered the question. "Of course she is. We have a baby to celebrate." Tucking her arm in Christine's, she led the way toward the entrance to the hall.

Taken aback, Christine saw no recourse except to follow. But she didn't have to stay long, she consoled herself. After one quick cup of coffee, she could escape. In the meantime, however, she might have an opportunity to quiz Marge a bit about the sheriff. A couple of discreet questions, that was all. Motivated by simple curiosity, nothing more.

Luck—or fate—was on her side. As they stepped into the hall, Marge drew her off to one side, leaving the others to descend on the long table where the coffee and donuts were being served.

"I have to help serve or my name will be mud, but would you mind doing me a big favor?" Marge waved at the women behind the table and held up her index finger, signaling she'd be over in a minute.

"Sure. If I can."

"I was going to call you about this later today, so it seems providential that you came to services. I'm in the ladies auxiliary here at church, and somehow I got roped into putting together a speaker's series for this year. Thank goodness, the year's almost up.

"Anyway, my speaker for November bailed on me yesterday. As I was considering replacements, it occurred to me that people would be interested in a talk on organic farming, what with the popularity of natural food and all. Can I twist your arm to fill in? It's the last Tuesday in November."

"I've never given a talk on my work. Or done much public speaking." Christine gave her a dubious look.

"But you should, my dear. It's a great way to promote the farm, especially in the off season when things are quiet. It would help build up interest and a customer base. I can think of any number of organizations in the area that would love to have you speak. And you do story hour every week. If you can hold the interest of a dozen youngsters, you'll have no problem with adults. What do you think?"

It wasn't a bad idea, Christine admitted. If she wanted the farm to keep growing, she'd have to find ways to advertise. And Marge was right about the quiet off season being a good opportunity to focus on promotion.

"I suppose I could give it a try."

"Wonderful! I think we'll draw both men and women to this one. I bet a lot of the farmers in the area would like to know more about their organic counterparts. And I know Cara will be there, her being a chef and all. Sam will be interested, too, with his health and medical background. We might even get the sheriff to drop in."

This was her opening, Christine realized. Adopting a casual stance, she angled away from the crowd. "He seems pretty busy with Jenna. It can't be easy being a single dad."

"Yes. Such a sad story. Married his college sweetheart. She was an actress, you know. In Hollywood. That's why Dale was in L.A. for almost a dozen years."

"What happened to her?"

"The way I understand it, she…"

"Would you like some coffee, Christine?"

The sound of Dale's voice close to her ear brought a flush to Christine's cheeks. How embarrassing to be caught making furtive inquiries about his past! Marge, however, didn't seem the least bothered by his sudden appearance.

"That's very nice of you, Dale. We want Christine to feel welcome so she'll come again. Meanwhile, I have to get to work. Thank you again for your help, my dear." Marge patted Christine's arm. "I'll be in touch with the details."

Although she would have liked to sink into the floor, Christine knew that wasn't an option. Taking the cup Dale offered, she kept her gaze downcast. "Thanks."

"I put in lots of cream, the way you like it."

"Thanks." She sounded like a stuck record. But if

she confined her responses to monosyllables, maybe he'd go away.

No such luck. He propped a shoulder against the wall, settling in. "My wife was killed in an accident on a movie set. A car went out of control during a chase scene and slid into the crowd of extras. She was the only casualty."

The words were matter-of-fact, but Christine heard the distant echo of pain behind them. Forcing herself to lift her head, she managed to find her voice. "I'm sorry."

"Thanks."

"I didn't mean to pry."

"No?" Tilting his head, he regarded her with a skeptical expression. "Those were pretty pointed questions you were asking Marge."

"I'm sorry." Guilt deepened the flush in her cheeks.

He took a measured sip of his coffee. "I don't mind. The details of my wife's death are no secret. Not much is in a small town. But turnabout seems fair play. If you can ask questions about me, I think I should be able to ask a few about you."

"Like what?" Her mouth went dry, and she moistened her lips.

"Like, why do you get nervous every time someone in uniform comes close?"

Recalling another old saying about offense being the best defense, she figured it was worth a try. "Did you ever think it might just be you, Sheriff?"

"At first. But Marv tells me you were the same with him."

Checkmate. Okay, perhaps a small dose of honesty would satisfy him, she strategized, regrouping. "I don't like cops."

"Why not? We're the good guys, remember?"

His tone had been light and teasing, but cynicism hardened her features and she gave a short, bitter laugh. "Yeah, right."

Her harsh, hostile response chased away every trace of humor in Dale's face. All at once, some of the pieces of the puzzle began to drop into place. She seemed like a decent, law-abiding citizen. Yet she had a record. And she hated cops. A frown creased his brow as he considered a new possibility, one that left a sick feeling in the pit of his stomach. When he spoke, his voice was somber. "Tell me about the DUI, Christine."

She drew in a sharp breath, as if she'd been slapped. "You checked my record."

"I wondered about alcohol the night you had the accident. I didn't see any evidence of it, but given your odd behavior, I thought it merited some follow-up." Not quite the whole truth about his reasons for delving into her past, but as much as he was willing to reveal.

"Then you saw everything else, too." Shock gave way to anger, and bright spots of color burned in her cheeks.

"Once I pulled up your file, it was all there."

A knot formed in Christine's stomach, tightening until it produced a physical pain. She'd thought she'd left the past behind, in Dunlap. But it had followed her here. She hadn't escaped the whole sordid mess after all. Her hopes for a fresh start were dissolving before her eyes, like sparkling fireworks that briefly light up a dark summer night but leave deeper blackness in their wake.

Choking back a sob, she set her cup on an adjacent table and almost ran from the hall, ignoring the curious looks that were cast in her direction. This was why she'd never let anyone get close. The risk of exposure was too great. And now she was paying the price for her lapse. Pretty soon, everyone in Oak Hill would know about the lawbreaker who ran Fresh Start Farm.

She heard steps pounding on the pavement behind her as she ran across the parking lot—and they were gaining fast. The safety of her truck was still yards away when Dale's hand closed around her arm.

"Christine, please wait. I'm sorry."

With a violent jerk, she pulled away from his grasp and turned, glaring. For several seconds it was a standoff as they stared at each other, her features tense with anguish, his etched with regret and concern.

"What are you going to do now, Sheriff?" Her chest heaving with exertion and distress, Christine broke the silence. "Charge me with resisting arrest? You'll know from my record that I've been down that road once. And then what? Are you going to throw me in jail? Do a strip search? I've been there, too."

As her choked words registered, a powerful, cold anger sent a chill through Dale and his eyes narrowed. "You were strip searched?" The quiet menace in his tone was almost more dangerous than a raised voice.

"Yes." At the memory of that degrading and frightening experience, Christine's cheeks lost their heightened color.

"Strip searches aren't common in small towns."

"Tell that to the sheriff in Dunlap."

A muscle twitched in his jaw. "Who did the search, Christine?" He had a feeling he already knew.

"He did. The sheriff."

Her barely audible response confirmed his suspicion—and stoked his anger. A strip search by an opposite-gender officer was a gross violation of police protocol.

"Did you tell anyone about this? What about your husband?"

Her combination of bitter laughter and tears unnerved him. "Trust me, he knew."

None of this was making sense. And the church parking lot wasn't the place to sort it out. "Look, let's go somewhere we can talk. My mother will watch Jenna."

"There's nothing to talk about, Sheriff." She backed away from him.

"I think there is. Police harassment is a criminal offense."

"Not in Dunlap." She drew a long, shaky breath. When she continued, her voice was more controlled. "And just for the record, none of those charges you found are true. I told you once I don't drink. I never have. That was a trumped-up accusation, the test results falsified. And yes, I resisted arrest, because I'd done nothing wrong. I paid for that with the humiliation of a strip search, a night in jail and the promise of worse if I ever got out of line again. As for the parking and speeding tickets—also bogus."

"But why, Christine? Why would the police harass you?" His mind whirling, Dale's intense gaze locked on hers. It never occurred to him not to believe her.

"It wasn't the police, plural. It was the sheriff. As for why…let's just say he was on my husband's un-official payroll."

She turned and walked to her truck, looking back once for a charged moment before she slid inside and drove away.

But in that brief glance, Dale saw a world of pain and disillusion. Along with a poignant vulnerability that hadn't been there until now. And that was his fault, he acknowledged with a pang. He'd dredged up the past she'd taken such efforts to escape, tainted her new life, soured her fresh start.

Dale felt like someone had kicked him in the gut. He'd just hurt a woman who had endured more than her share of hurt already. If he could, he'd rewind and delete the past fifteen minutes.

Unfortunately, it was too late for that. But it wasn't too late to pursue justice. Christine had been wronged. There was no doubt in his mind that she'd told him the truth. Yet for whatever reason, she'd been unable to fight her foes. Something—or someone—had tied her hands.

Well, *his* hands weren't tied. Nor was it too late to see that justice was done.

Starting right now.

Chapter Ten

To her credit, his mother didn't pepper Dale with queries when he asked if she could watch Jenna for a few hours. Having witnessed Christine's quick exit, she posed just one question. "What's wrong?"

"I don't know." His mouth settled into a grim line. "But I'm going to try and find out."

"Take your time. Jenna and I will make cookies."

On days like this, Dale was reminded why he'd moved home. And how much he loved his mother. He managed a small smile and leaned over to kiss her cheek. "Thanks, Mom."

"No thanks necessary. You just get busy and do what it takes to help that young woman. I have a feeling she could use a friend."

Now, two hours later, Dale leaned back in his desk chair and frowned at the computer screen. He'd ditched his suit jacket and loosened his tie as soon as he'd arrived in his office, trying to get comfortable.

But the information he'd uncovered hadn't helped him achieve that goal. In fact, it made him decidedly uncomfortable.

After fifteen years in law enforcement, Dale was convinced that the vast majority of cops were conscientious, trustworthy public servants. But isolated cases of corruption did exist. And based on his research so far, it seemed he'd found one such glaring case in Dunlap, Nebraska.

As Christine had told him, every official document in her record was signed by Sheriff Gary Stratton—despite the fact that Dunlap had two part-time deputies. The odds that all of the alleged violations would be documented by the sheriff were small…unless Christine had been set up, as she claimed.

The personal data on Stratton had taken a little longer to dig up, but it had also revealed some suspicious information. Age forty-four and divorced with no children, the man lived in an expensive home and drove a BMW. Not a lifestyle that could be supported by a small-town sheriff's salary, unless his public service income was supplemented by family money. In this case, it wasn't. Stratton had grown up on a small farm in upstate Nebraska, which had been sold to pay inheritance taxes after his father died eight years before.

So where was his money coming from?

One possibility was Jack Barlow. Christine had said the sheriff was on her husband's payroll. But why would her own husband want to harass his wife? And why would the sheriff go along with it?

His frown deepening, Dale dug into the personal data on Barlow. Age forty-two at his death and president of Barlow Equipment, an agricultural machinery dealer, he'd attended a prestigious college in the East and was active in church and civic organizations. Nothing in the documentation suggested the man was anything less than a leading citizen of the town.

The local newspaper might offer some additional information, Dale reflected, as he keyed into the online archives of the *Dunlap Messenger.* He typed in the name *Jack Barlow,* and a flood of headlines popped up in reverse chronological order. Most were innocuous. Barlow speaking at a regional farmers' meeting, handing over a donation to a local philanthropic organization, attending a charity event. Dale focused on the final two stories, which dealt with his sudden death and funeral.

The funeral story provided nothing but a rundown of the facts and a few quotes from the eulogies. The story on his sudden death in the crash of the small plane he was piloting offered more—including one very pertinent piece of information. The other casualty was his sole passenger, a Candace Decker, age twenty-eight and a clerk in the legal department at Barlow Equipment. According to the article, a flight plan indicated they'd been heading for Las Vegas.

As a cop, Dale knew that jumping to conclusions

was dangerous. But he'd be willing to bet Barlow and his companion hadn't been going to Vegas on company business. And he was also certain this latest piece of information was relevant to Christine's situation. But how? And where did Stratton fit into the picture?

He typed Gary Stratton's name into the newspaper archives. The three most recent headlines, again in reverse chronological order and spaced out over the past four months, confirmed Dale's suspicion that the man was one of the rare corrupt cops.

"Court To Consider Plea Bargain In Stratton Case"
"Interim Sheriff Appointed In Dunlap"
"Local Sheriff Indicted For Graft"

According to the articles, Stratton's illegal activities had been exposed by his newest deputy, who'd witnessed the handoff of a pack of cigarettes and had later found the pack—stuffed with cash—in Stratton's desk. His suspicions already aroused by other irregularities in the department, the man had taken his concerns to the county prosecuting attorney. Stratton had been suspended from duty while an investigation took place.

The final story suggested that Stratton had been taking bribes for years from several individuals and businesses. In exchange for identifying those who'd paid him off, he was plea bargaining for a reduced sentence.

While the names of those who'd purchased his favors weren't revealed in the newspaper, Dale knew Jack Barlow was among them. But Barlow was dead. If Stratton's attorney was smart, he'd advise his client to keep Barlow's name to himself. Assuming no paper trail existed, there would be nothing to tie him to Christine's husband—and to yet another incriminating example of graft. Nor would there be a way to prove that the charges against Christine had been false. Without such proof, it would be difficult, if not impossible, to expunge her record. And Dale wasn't willing to settle for anything less.

He wasn't sure what it would take to put things right in this situation. He did know it wouldn't be easy. But he also knew he wasn't going to back off until her name was cleared. Obtaining justice for Christine had become a personal fight.

As for why…that was yet one more unanswered question on his growing list. A list that included another equally troubling question.

Why hadn't Christine fought back?

"You're sure you'll be okay while I'm gone?"

Smiling, Dale bent and kissed his mother's cheek as he and Jenna prepared to leave her at the security checkpoint in Lambert—St. Louis International Airport. "We'll be fine, Mom. We'll miss you a lot, but we'll get by."

"I could still cancel my trip. Lillian would understand."

"No way. In the two years I've been back in Oak Hill, you haven't taken a single trip. You need a vacation, and you can't disappoint Aunt Lillian."

"I suppose you're right." The woman stooped to hug her granddaughter. "You be good for your daddy while I'm gone, okay?"

"I will. I love you, Grandma."

"I love you, too, honey." She directed her next comment to Dale. "Call me if you need me to come back early."

"Scout's honor." Grinning, he raised his hand. "Give Aunt Lillian a hug for me."

"I will." With a wave, Arlene joined the security line.

A few minutes later, a quick glance at his daughter's bereft expression as her grandmother disappeared in the crowd headed for the gates convinced Dale that diversionary tactics were in order. "What do you say we get hamburgers and French fries for lunch on the way home?"

"Could we?" She looked up at him, her eyes shining. Fast food was a rare treat.

"Mmm-hmm. I think this would be a good day for a splurge."

Fifteen minutes later, Dale pulled off the highway at a familiar burger chain. Their order was filled with the usual assembly line efficiency of such places, and as he divvied up the food and unwrapped Jenna's burger, she dipped a French fry into her ketchup and smiled at him.

"This is more fun than eating at home, Daddy."

"Are you saying you don't like my cooking? My heart is broken."

His exaggerated theatrics elicited a giggle. "You cook good. I like your meat loaf best."

"That's one of my favorites, too."

"Where did you learn how to cook it?"

His hand stilled for a brief instant as he opened a packet of ketchup. "Your mommy used to make it. I have her recipe."

"I wish I could remember her." Jenna's face grew wistful.

"I do, too, honey." The last word came out raspy, and he cleared his throat.

"Ms. Christine read a story yesterday at story hour about a little boy who didn't have a mommy, either. But he found one in the end. Do you think that might happen for me?"

"I don't know, Jenna." Dale's appetite was vanishing as fast as an ice cube on a hot summer day, leaving a hollow feeling in the pit of his stomach. The lack of a mother in Jenna's life was one of his greatest regrets.

"Ms. Christine would be a good mommy. She has a pretty smile, and she listens when I talk, and she smells real good. I think about her a lot."

So did he, Dale reflected—for very different reasons. In fact, he'd thought of little else since their confrontation on the church parking lot four days ago. Although he'd continued to dig for information in the interim, he'd learned little more. But after calling in some favors among his friends in law enforcement, he'd confirmed that the Dunlap sheriff hadn't named Jack Barlow as one of the people who'd paid him off. Nevertheless, Dale had shared his suspicions with the prosecuting attorney on the case, who'd promised to look into the matter.

"Don't you think so, Daddy?"

"Think what, honey?" With an effort, Dale tried to refocus on the conversation.

"That Ms. Christine would be a good mommy."

He kept his tone neutral. "I suppose so."

"Why couldn't she be my mommy?"

"It's not that easy, honey. I'd have to marry her first."

"If you did, she'd live with us, right?"

"That's right."

"What's wrong with that? Don't you like her?"

A bite of burger stuck in his throat, and he swallowed with difficulty. "She seems very nice. But when you marry someone, it means you'll stay with them for the rest of your life. That's a long time. So you have to be very sure you like that person a whole lot."

"I like Ms. Christine a whole lot."

How had they gotten into this conversation? Dale wondered. And how was he going to get out of it?

"Are you all finished, honey?"

She looked down at her food. "I still have some French fries."

"I'll tell you what. Let's wrap them up and you can eat them in the car on the way home."

"I thought I wasn't supposed to eat in the car."

"Just for today we'll make an exception."

"What's a 'ception?"

"It's when the person who made a rule tells you it's okay to break it."

"But why is it okay?"

As he gathered up his almost untouched food, Dale prayed for guidance. "Because it's a long drive home and I promised Deputy Wallace I'd stop in and see him as soon as I got back."

"But what about your lunch? You always told me not to waste food." She gave him a disapproving look as he started to stuff his burger into the bag with the trash. "Is that another 'ception?"

"No." Withdrawing his hand, Dale rewrapped the burger with more care. "I'm taking this home to eat later. Now tell me what you did in preschool yesterday. Grandma said you learned about Thanksgiving."

As they exited the restaurant and he strapped her in, setting the French fries in her lap, Jenna chattered about preschool. He said a silent prayer of thanks that children could be easily distracted.

He only wished the same were true for him.

But try as he might, he couldn't seem to get a certain auburn-haired woman with soft brown eyes out of his mind.

Double-checking the address, Christine pulled up in front of Dale's tiny bungalow on a quiet street in Oak Hill. On a Friday morning, no one should be home. Arlene had told her that Jenna attended preschool on Monday, Wednesday and Friday until noon, and Dale would be at work.

She'd tried calling Arlene on Wednesday after she'd found her checkbook pushed halfway under a row of shelving in the library. The woman must have dropped it during story hour, Christine had concluded. Then she'd remembered Arlene mentioning a trip to the Southwest to visit her sister. Christine had no idea how to reach her, but Dale would. She'd discarded the notion of calling and leaving a message, unwilling to take the chance he'd answer. Nor had she wanted to drop by the sheriff's office and see him face-to-face. The safest course of action was to leave it inside his mailbox with a note.

Wrapping her sweater around her to ward off the unseasonable chill, she picked up the manila envelope containing the checkbook and slid from her truck. To her relief, the box was on the street rather than by the front door, meaning she didn't have to approach the house. Pulling open the small door, she slipped the envelope inside, prepared to make a fast exit.

But as she turned to go a flutter at the curtains in the front window caught her attention. That was odd. No one should be home at this hour.

Before she had a chance to ponder the situation, the front door opened. Jenna was framed in the opening, still in her pajamas at eleven in the morning. Was she sick? Christine wondered. And if she was, who was taking care of her?

Without hesitating, she strode down the front walk toward the little girl. The closer she got, the more concerned she became. Jenna's pale cheeks were tear streaked, and she was trembling. Dropping down to her level, Christine smoothed the hair back from her forehead and gave her a comforting hug.

"Jenna, honey, what's wrong? Are you sick?"

"N-no. But daddy is."

Looking over the little girl's shoulder into the tiny living room, Christine saw no sign of Dale. "Where is he?"

"I— in the bathroom."

Torn, Christine debated her next move. She was pretty sure Dale wouldn't appreciate her interference. Yet she couldn't ignore Jenna's distress. As she stroked the little girl's back, trying to figure out the best way to handle the situation, Dale stepped into the living room from the hall. And after one look at him, she knew she couldn't walk away.

Bent slightly, his white-knuckled grip on the door frame suggesting he needed the support to remain upright, he appeared to be in severe discomfort. A permanent grimace seemed to be etched on his colorless face, and despite the cool day, his hair was damp, as was the T-shirt that hugged his muscular chest.

Standing, Christine kept one hand on Jenna's shoulder. "You look terrible! Have you called Dr. Martin?"

"I'll be okay. What are you doing here?"

"Your mother dropped her checkbook at the library. I was putting it in your mailbox when Jenna came to the door."

As a sudden spasm of pain tightened his features and he drew in a sharp breath, panic clutched at Christine. Dale had always radiated a quiet, reliable strength. To see him hurting and vulnerable was more than unsettling; it scared her to death.

Without waiting for an invitation, she moved into the house, stopping inches away from him. "If you aren't going to call Dr. Martin, I am."

"He threw up. A bunch of times," Jenna offered. "I wanted to call Grandma, but he wouldn't let me."

Uncharacteristic irritation flared in Dale's eyes. "Jenna, go read your book while I talk to Ms. Christine."

"I think you should call Dr. Martin, too." The mutinous set of his daughter's chin reminded Christine of the sheriff.

"Look, I don't need you two ganging up on me. I…" All at once he clutched his stomach, and without another word he headed down the hall. Fast. A few seconds later, the muffled sound of someone being violently sick permeated the house.

Dropping onto one knee beside Jenna, Christine tried to keep the alarm that had set every nerve in her body on edge from seeping into her voice. "When did your daddy get sick?"

"This morning. He was fixing my breakfast, and all of a sudden he got real white, like a ghost, and ran down the hall."

At least his illness was very recent, Christine thought in relief. "It sounds like the flu to me. It's not very much fun, but after a few days it goes away and you feel fine again. I'm going to call Dr. Martin, though, in case he wants to give your daddy some medicine to help him feel better faster. Why don't you sit down and look at that book you took home from the library, about the magic school bus? And after I call Dr. Martin, we'll see about having some lunch. How does that sound?"

"Okay, I guess." The little girl's lower lip quivered. "But I'm scared. Daddy's never been sick."

Her throat constricting with emotion, Christine pulled the little girl close. "You don't need to be scared anymore. We'll take good care of him, okay?"

"I'm glad you came over." Sniffling, Jenna tightened her grip on Christine.

"Me, too. Now you go get that book while I call Dr. Martin."

By the time Dale emerged from the bathroom, shaken and weak, Christine had placed the call. Sam was seeing his last patient of the morning and had promised to run over on his lunch hour as soon as he finished.

"Dr. Martin will be here in a few minutes." Christine met him in the hall.

The intimidating glare Dale gave her had little impact, considering he was using a door frame to hold himself up.

"What is this, some macho male thing?" Christine propped her hands on her hips and glared back. "You're sick. And even if you want to try and tough this out, you have a very frightened little daughter to think about. You need to do this for her if not for yourself. So will you please get back into bed before you fall on your face?"

As she concluded her tirade, Dale's defiance changed to shock. Then, to her surprise, a glint of humor sparked in his eyes. "Did anyone ever tell you that you're bossy?"

Although she'd been prepared to argue her point, Christine was glad she didn't have to. It seemed Dale was going to capitulate. Some of the tension melted from her shoulders, and she lifted her chin. "Headstrong, maybe. Never bossy. Most of the time I'm quite reasonable."

"I might debate that, but I'm not up to it at the

moment." He wiped the sleeve of his shirt against his damp forehead.

Without thinking, she moved closer and laid a hand on his forehead. His skin was clammy beneath her fingers, and hot. Too hot. "You're burning up. Where's your thermometer?"

"In the medicine cabinet in the bathroom. But don't bother. I already checked. A hundred and two."

"You must have the flu."

"Nope." He pushed off from the door frame and started down the hall, steadying himself against the wall as he moved slowly down the short length, every step an obvious effort.

"How do you know?" she called after him, confused.

"I have a pretty good idea what's wrong."

When he didn't offer more, Christine followed him, distracted for a brief second as she passed Jenna's pink and mauve bedroom, with its fairy-tale princess border and white furniture. "Do you want to let me in on the secret?"

"Food poisoning."

"Why do you think that?" Twin furrows appeared on her brow.

"All the evidence points in that direction."

She let out her breath in a huff. "Could you stop being a cop for five minutes and explain your conclusion in plain English?"

He eased himself down on the bed, wincing a bit as he sat. Christine came to an abrupt halt on the threshold of the austere room, which contained only a queen-sized bed, a dresser and a chair.

"In plain English, Jenna and I stopped for burgers in St. Louis after we dropped my mom off at the airport yesterday. I brought most of mine home and forgot to refrigerate it. When I got hungry about ten o'clock last night, I ate it. Not the smartest thing I've ever done."

"You ate ground beef that had been sitting out for what… ten hours?"

"I nuked it first. A little."

Shaking her head, Christine rolled her eyes. "Lie down, Dale. We'll let Dr. Martin deal with this. I'm going to see how Jenna's doing."

By the time Sam rang the bell twenty minutes later, Dale had made two more trips down the hall. If she didn't feel so sorry for him, Christine would have given him a lecture on food-handling techniques. Except she figured he knew he'd been stupid and felt foolish enough already. Since he didn't strike her as the kind of guy who made many mistakes in judgment, she had to assume he'd been seriously preoccupied. She could think of no other reason for such a lapse.

Pulling the door open, Christine ushered Sam in. "I seem to be calling you a lot lately, Dr. Martin. Thanks for coming."

"I think we know each other well enough by now

to switch to first names, don't you?" One corner of his mouth hitched up.

"I guess we do."

"So what's the problem with Dale? He never gets sick."

As she relayed the sheriff's self-diagnosis, Sam nodded. "Sounds like he's right on the money. But you never know. It could be something else. Where is he?"

"In the bedroom."

As he started down the hall, he paused long enough to smile at Jenna. "How are you today, princess?"

"I'm fine. But daddy's real sick."

"Well, we're going to fix him all up."

While he examined Dale, Christine kept Jenna occupied by reading her one of the books Arlene had checked out of the library. When Sam stepped into the hall ten minutes later, closing the door behind him, she popped in a video and left Jenna to enjoy the on-screen adventure while she dealt with the real-life drama.

"I think he's right." Sam kept his voice low as Christine joined him in the hall. "He has all the classic symptoms of salmonella, and they're on the severe side. My biggest concern is dehydration. If he continues to lose fluids at this rate we'll need to think about electrolyte replacement."

"How serious is this?" Christine tried to suppress her anxiety, but a slight tremor ran through her words.

"It can be very dangerous, especially for older

people, young children and those with impaired immune systems. The good news is that Dale doesn't fall into any of those categories. Plus, he's in great shape. However, his life isn't going to be too pleasant for the next couple of days, and I expect he'll be tired for several more days after that. It's unfortunate his mother is on vacation. He's not up to taking care of himself, let alone Jenna."

"I wonder if he'd let me help?" Christine wasn't sure where that idea had come from, but Sam seemed to take it in stride.

"It might be worth suggesting. Dale isn't the kind of guy who likes to admit he needs help, but in this case, he does. And if the offer comes from a friend, he might be more inclined to take it."

"We're not exactly friends." Warmth stole onto her cheeks.

"That's odd." A quizzical expression flitted over Sam's features. "I had a different impression just now from Dale."

Although she was tempted to ask him to explain that comment, Christine figured such a request would fuel speculation. Better to let it pass. "I suppose it can't hurt to offer."

"If he's smart, he won't turn you down."

As Christine showed the doctor out, she considered Sam's comment. Dale *was* smart. Meaning that in light of their tempestuous relationship, he might consider it wise to refuse her offer. Why would he want a woman who'd treated him with hostility hanging around his house, taking care of him and his daughter?

But a more disturbing question followed closely on the heels of that one.

Why would she want to offer?

Concern for Jenna's well-being was one reason, of course. But if she was honest with herself, Christine knew it wasn't the only one. Or even the primary one.

The main reason was Dale himself.

Because as much as she hated to admit it, and as much as it scared her, Oak Hill's sheriff had somehow managed to breach the barriers around her heart.

Chapter Eleven

"Is daddy sleeping?"

Tiptoeing down the hall, Christine smiled at an anxious Jenna. "Yes. And that's a good thing. The more he rests, the faster he'll get better."

"Are you really going to stay here with us all night?" Jenna eyed the overnight bag Christine had left in the hall after she'd returned from a quick trip home and to the grocery store with the youngster in tow.

"Yes. It will be like a slumber party." Dale's quick acceptance of her offer was one more indication of how sick he was.

"Can we stay up late and watch a bunch of movies?"

"Not too late. We've both had a long day. But one movie would be okay."

"I like *Beauty and the Beast*."

"That sounds good to me—after we have some dinner."

As Christine moved about Dale's tiny kitchen,

sharing giggles with Jenna while the youngster "helped" her, a wistful longing tightened her throat. This was what she'd always wanted…a home of her own, filled with love and laughter and the voices of children. Though she'd given up that dream, being in Dale's house reminded her of what could have been had her marriage to Jack been all she'd hoped.

Even after everything that had happened, she found it hard to believe she'd been so easily duped. Until Jack, her instincts about people had always been sound. But that error in judgment had shaken her confidence. If she'd been wrong about him, how could she ever be sure about anyone? As a result, walking a wide circle around men in general—and sheriffs in particular—seemed the prudent thing to do. If loneliness was the price she had to pay to protect her heart, it was well worth it.

At least it had been, until a certain sheriff with an angelic, blond-haired daughter had stepped into her life and undermined her resolve. Dale's honor and integrity appeared to be as real and sincere as Jenna's innocence and enthusiasm. But appearances could be deceiving. And she'd made one big mistake. She couldn't afford to make another.

"The biscuits smell good, Ms. Christine."

Reining in her wayward thoughts, she smiled at the little girl. "I always bake biscuits on special occasions."

"Is this a special occasion?"

"Of course. It's not every day that I get to have dinner with the prettiest little girl in Oak Hill."

A grin brightened Jenna's face. "We have biscuits sometimes. But they come in a can."

"Those are good, too. But I got this recipe from my mother, and it's even better."

"We have some recipes from my mommy." Jenna carried a glass of water to the table, holding it with both hands. "My daddy fixes her meat loaf every week. I don't remember her, though. She died when I was little."

"My mommy died, too."

"Do you miss her?" Turning from the table, Jenna regarded her with solemn eyes.

"All the time."

With a sigh, Jenna went back to setting the table. "I asked Daddy if I could get a new mommy, like that little boy in the book you read at story hour, but he said it wouldn't be easy. I guess that means no." She studied Christine, her expression hopeful as she climbed onto her chair. "You'd be a good mommy."

Christine swallowed past the sudden lump in her throat as she cut up some chicken on Jenna's plate. "Thank you, honey."

"I told Daddy I wished you were *my* mommy."

Taking her seat, Christine tried to suppress the warm flush that crept up her neck and spilled onto her cheeks. Dale must have loved that, she mused.

"He kind of looked the way you look now when I

told him that." Jenna speared a piece of meat and twirled it on her fork as she watched Christine.

Deciding that a change of subject was in order, Christine buttered a biscuit and set it on Jenna's plate. "Let's eat up or everything will get cold."

"Aren't we going to pray first?"

Feeling chastised, Christine lowered her fork to the table. For most of her life, she wouldn't have considered eating without offering thanks to God first. But she'd gotten out of the habit in the past two years. "Of course. Would you like to say the prayer?"

"Okay." Jenna folded her hands and bowed her head. "Thank you for this good food, God. And thank you for sending Ms. Christine to our house today. Please help Daddy get well real fast. And please bless all the people in the world who are hungry tonight. Amen."

With Christine steering the conversation, they managed to avoid colliding with any more embarrassing topics during the meal. Later, after the kitchen was put back in order, they snuggled on the couch, an afghan thrown over them as they watched the movie. Christine kept one ear tuned to Dale's bedroom, but she'd learned that he didn't like to be fussed over when he was sick. Other than refilling his water pitcher and encouraging him to keep drinking, she'd respected his privacy.

The good news was that the frequency of his trips down the hall to the bathroom had declined quite a bit, and he was sleeping a lot. She suspected that in a day or two he'd be well on the road to recovery.

As the movie progressed, Jenna's eyelids began to droop. Easing her closer, Christine put her arm around the little girl, enjoying the warm, trusting little body close to hers. Stroking Jenna's hair, she pressed a soft kiss to the top of her head, savoring the moment and enjoying this brief, tantalizing taste of motherhood.

By the movie's halfway point, Jenna gave up the fight to stay awake. Christine reduced the volume and, lulled by the background noise, she also grew drowsy. Long before the final credits ran, she, too, had surrendered to sleep.

Jenna's bed was empty.

For an instant, a suffocating panic swept over Dale as he scanned her room. And then he remembered. He was sick. Christine was taking care of Jenna. But why wasn't his daughter in bed? He'd checked the clock on his nightstand, and it was way past her bedtime.

Padding down the hall to the living room, his bare feet soundless on the carpet, he solved the mystery in one glance. The TV set was on, the screen a blank blue, as if a video had run out. Across from it, on the couch, Jenna was snuggled up against Christine. Both of them were sound asleep.

Jenna looked adorable, as always. But it was Christine who drew his attention. Her head was tilted a bit toward Jenna and tipped back, exposing the delicate curve of her throat. Dale had never seen her look more relaxed. Gone was the taut wariness that stiffened her features and tensed her body, giving the impression that she was poised to flee at the slightest hint of danger. Her lips were pliant and full, her breathing deep and regular, the soft mohair of her forest-green sweater rising and falling in an even cadence. One stocking-footed, jeans-clad leg was tucked under her, and Jenna lay sprawled against her side.

Tenderness tightened Dale's throat as he gazed at them. They looked good together, the auburn-haired woman and the blond little girl. And comfortable. Under different circumstances, he'd be inclined to consider Jenna's idea about drafting Christine as her new mommy. After all, his daughter wasn't the only one who found the mystery lady appealing.

But she had problems. Big ones, from what he could gather. Not just in terms of the law, but on a personal level. The trauma that had made her wary had left serious scars that could affect her—and whoever became involved with her—for the rest of their lives.

Dale had been down that road. And much as he was growing to care for Christine, he couldn't let himself get too close to another fragile, damaged woman. He'd do what he could to expunge her police record. And he'd pray that the Lord would help her heal once she was free of her past. But he couldn't do anything more, no matter how much his daughter wanted a mother. And no matter how attracted he was to the woman who looked so at home in his living room.

Fortifying his resolve, he crossed the room and reached for Jenna, doing his best to extricate her from the circle of Christine's arms without waking either.

He succeeded with Jenna, but Christine stirred. For a moment she seemed disoriented—and alarmed to find him bending close to her. Blinking away slumber, she sucked in a sharp breath and pulled back.

"It's okay. You both fell asleep. I'm going to put Jenna to bed." Dale kept his voice low and reassuring as he cupped his daughter's head against his shoulder and straightened up.

"You shouldn't be out of bed. I can take her." Christine started to rise, but when she tried to stand on the leg that had been tucked under her she lurched toward him.

Keeping a firm clasp on Jenna, Dale grabbed Christine's arm to steady her.

"My leg went to sleep," she whispered, trying without much success to put her weight on it.

"Just sit tight till I get back. In my present condition, I can't support both of you." Dale flashed her a brief grin, then disappeared down the hall.

When he returned, Christine was perched on the edge of the couch, her leg stretched out in front of her as she wiggled her foot.

She scrutinized him as he approached. "How are you feeling?"

"Better than this morning."

"I don't think that would be too difficult."

"True." Quiet descended in the dim room, and he wished he had pockets in his sweatpants. It would give him something to do with his hands, which suddenly felt awkward. For lack of any other options, he picked up the remote and turned off the TV. The room went dark, masking expressions, and he relaxed a bit. "Listen, I want to thank you for all you did today. I'm sorry if I was a bit grumpy earlier. I don't handle being sick very well."

"So I discovered."

He listened for resentment in her tone, but to his surprise he heard a touch of wry humor instead. "I also appreciate your offer to stay tonight, but it's not necessary. I'll be okay, and I doubt Jenna will wake up until morning."

"You didn't look too steady carrying her down the hall."

He couldn't dispute her observation. His feather-weight daughter had felt like a stack of concrete blocks in his arms. Dale had had the flu a few years back, and it had left him weak and shaky. But this was far worse. In truth, he'd welcome the presence of an able-bodied adult overnight. And Christine's was the sole offer he'd had.

When he didn't respond at once, Christine rose. Even in the dim light, he could see from her posture that the familiar stiffness was back. "I don't want to intrude. I'll get my things."

As she started to brush past him, he grasped her arm.

He hadn't meant to offend her, but now that she was inches away, he could see the hurt in the depths of her brown eyes. "You're not intruding, Christine." His words were soft, her name on his lips a mere whisper.

He couldn't read her shadowy face, but he felt a tremor run through her. At the sudden current that sizzled between them, his heart stopped, then raced on. His gaze dropped to her slightly parted lips and his mouth went dry as a yearning surged inside him, tempting him to close the distance between them and taste her lips, touch her soft hair, hold her close. The urge was so strong that he leaned a bit toward her and began to lift his other arm.

Then fate intervened—in the form of salmonella. All at once his stomach twisted into a knot, and without another word he stepped around her and hot-footed it down the hall.

She was standing by the front door when he reappeared a few minutes later, her overnight case on the floor beside her. She'd flipped on a light in the living room, dispelling the charged mood of a few minutes earlier, and her car keys were in her hand.

Eating crow had never been Dale's strong suit. But this last little episode had wiped him out, and his temperature hadn't yet dropped below one hundred. Like it or not, he needed help. "I've had some second thoughts."

"Are you worse? Should I call Sam?" Creases appeared on her brow.

"No. I think my symptoms are normal, given the diagnosis." He leaned against the wall, needing the support. "But this thing has knocked me flat. I'd feel better if someone else was here, for Jenna's sake. I just hate for you to have to sleep on the couch."

"It's no big deal. I've spent far less comfortable nights."

If he was feeling up to par, Dale would have pursued that pain-rippled comment. As it was, all he wanted to do was lie down. "You'll stay, then?"

"Yes. Do you need help getting back to the bedroom?"

"I think I can manage. Thanks." His mouth quirked up at one corner, and with an effort he pushed off from the wall, doing his best not to sway. "I'll see you in the morning."

As he walked the length of the short hall, he knew Christine was watching him. Had she sensed that he'd wanted to kiss her? Her reaction had been impossible to discern in the darkness, but surely she'd felt the spark between them. Yet given their history, wouldn't she have pulled back if she had? She'd wanted no part of him up until now, and there was no reason to think her attitude had softened enough to allow for the possibility of romance. But how could she have been unaware of the powerful undercurrents?

Closing his door, Dale stretched out on his bed, every muscle in his body aching. And as sleep transported him to welcome oblivion, he concluded that

Christine couldn't have missed those vibrations. Yet, like him, she would fight them—for reasons he was beginning to understand.

But there were still far too many things he *didn't* understand about the mystery lady. And as soon as he got back on his feet, he was going to get some answers to his questions.

"If I never see another banana again, it will be too soon."

At Dale's morose expression, Christine burst out laughing. She wiped the dishcloth across the kitchen counter, gathering up the crumbs from the breakfast she'd prepared for Jenna before taking her to preschool.

"Hey, it's not funny," he protested. "How would you like to eat nothing but bananas, rice, applesauce and toast for days on end?"

"Doctor's orders. Sam said to stick to a soft, bland diet. And this is only the third day."

"It feels like a week."

"You could try a poached egg later." Smiling, she picked up her purse.

He rolled his eyes. "Wow. That's exciting." Surveying his half-eaten banana, he wrinkled his nose in distaste. "You know, I'm tempted to pay a visit to Gus's."

A look of horror swept over Christine's face. "If you do, count on a relapse. Deep-fried is that man's middle name."

"I'll have you know that since Cara opened the restaurant at the Oak Hill Inn, Gus had been featuring one healthy special every day."

"I don't think the words *Gus* and *healthy* belong in the same sentence."

"Well, it's his version of healthy," Dale amended. "Everything's still breaded, but he bakes it instead of frying it. The stuff's not half-bad for a quick meal."

"Trust me. Stick with the bland diet for now. Do you need anything else before I go?"

At her question, an odd light flared in Dale's eyes. It was a twin of the one she'd seen in the living room the night he'd gotten sick, and she felt her neck grow warm. But to her relief the glimmer faded as fast as it had appeared.

"You've already done more than enough, Christine."

"I don't mind. You came to my rescue on several occasions. I was glad to return the favor. Jenna gets picked up at noon, right?"

"Yes. But I can get her."

She shook her head. He'd improved a great deal, but the lines of fatigue on his face and the hollows in his cheeks were stark reminders of the ordeal his body had been through. And though he tried to be subtle about it, Christine noticed that he continued to hold on to every available surface when he walked.

Worried, she'd talked to Sam about it late yesterday, but he'd assured her that such weakness wasn't unusual, given the severity of Dale's infection. According to Sam, it could take Dale ten days to regain full strength and feel back to normal. Already, at eight-thirty in the morning, he looked spent.

"I'll do it today. Why don't you go back to bed for a while?"

"I just got up."

"You look like you shouldn't have."

"Gee, thanks. You're great for a guy's ego."

The teasing between them was new. It had developed over the weekend as Christine had popped in and out, checking on Dale and entertaining Jenna. And she was enjoying it.

"I do my best."

"Very funny." He nodded toward a mug he'd placed on the table. "I thought you might like a cup of coffee before you go."

She hesitated. Now that the farmers' markets were closed for the season and her garden was winding down, she had more leisure. And she was tempted to accept his invitation. But she wasn't sure it would be wise. The more she was around Dale, the more she liked him. And that wasn't a good thing. Not if she was determined to remain uninvolved.

"Stay for ten minutes, Christine," Dale cajoled. "I don't expect more than that. You've already given us far too much of your time. But a little company would be nice."

What could ten minutes hurt? she reasoned. Sip a cup of coffee, engage in a little small talk, send him back to bed. No risk there. "Okay."

He started to rise, but she pressed him back with a hand on his shoulder. "I'll get it."

"I'm not much of a host, am I?" He sank back without protest.

"You can make up for it another time." She moved to the counter and began to measure out the coffee.

"Is that a promise?"

The quiet question surprised her and she angled toward him, catching a quick glimpse of yearning before the corners of his lips lifted into a smile that seemed a bit forced. His tone was lighter when he spoke again. "I always pay my debts."

"You don't owe me anything, Dale. What I did simply evened things out."

"Is that why you offered to help? Because you felt you owed me?"

She couldn't answer that question while lost in those perceptive blue eyes. Turning back to the coffeemaker, she poured in the water, sorry now that she'd agreed to stay. "I don't like to be obligated to anyone," she hedged.

"Why not?"

Because they can control you and turn your life into a nightmare. But she didn't voice that response.

"I just prefer it that way. It's easier." *And safer.*

He ate the rest of his banana in silence while she

fiddled with the coffeemaker. When she joined him at the tiny round café table for two tucked against one wall, he could tell from the slight tremor in her hands as she lifted her mug that their conversation had touched a nerve. Why?

A discussion about her past hadn't been on Dale's agenda today, but all at once it seemed opportune. With Jenna at preschool, they'd have total privacy and no interruptions. Besides, the lighter mood had evaporated anyway.

Taking a sip of water, Dale folded his hands on the table. There was no easy way to lead up to this subject. Nothing he could do to pave the way and put her at ease. So he chose a direct approach.

"I have some news for you about Gary Stratton."

Her hand jerked, sloshing coffee on the table. Dale reached for his napkin and sopped up the spill, giving her a chance to recover and leaving the ball in her court. He would play this by ear, depending on how she reacted to his announcement.

The silence between them stretched, and he watched as her expression evolved from shock to wariness. Though she didn't move a muscle, he could feel her withdraw. Her lips grew taut and settled into a thin, straight line.

"I have no interest in Gary Stratton." The revulsion in her tone was chilling.

"I think you might want to hear this. It appears that his past has caught up with him." When that comment sparked a flash of interest, he continued. "Stratton has been charged with graft and removed from office. According to a recent story in the *Dunlap Messenger,* he's trying to plea bargain for a reduced sentence."

"But…Jack's been dead for more than a year." Confusion rippled across her features. "And I'm sure there's no evidence. How did he get caught?"

"It appears your husband wasn't alone in buying the good sheriff's favors."

"You mean…other people were bribing him, too?"

"Yes. I checked with the county prosecuting attorney. Your husband's name isn't among the ones Stratton has offered as a bargaining chip. At least, not yet. I shared parts of your story with the attorney, and he's going to do some checking. My goal is to get your record expunged."

Puzzled, she gave him an assessing look. "Why is that important to you?"

"As I told you weeks ago, I do my best to see that justice is done. You shouldn't have to live the rest of your life with a falsified police record." He hesitated, knowing he was moving onto very shaky ground, that there was a good chance she would close down. But there might never be a better opportunity to broach the subject of her past. "To get that done, though, we're going to have to prove that your husband paid off the sheriff."

"That's not going to happen." Her shoulders slumped. "Jack was very careful. I saw one payoff—

in cash—and I'm sure that's how he handled all of them. There won't be any documentation."

"How long did this go on, Christine?"

"A year."

"He might have gotten a little careless after a while. Going undetected for an extended period can breed sloppiness and complacency. Criminals get cocky and make mistakes."

"Not Jack. He was very thorough in everything." There was a bitter edge to her words.

"Your testimony alone could be helpful in implicating your husband. You witnessed one payoff. And Stratton's credibility is already compromised. The judge will be more likely to believe you than him."

She didn't look convinced. "I don't want to revisit all this, Dale."

"Even to clear your name?"

"I'm not sure."

Leaning back, Dale scrutinized her face. Anxiety pinched her features, and there was a suspicious sheen in her eyes. While he'd known her past was painful, it must have been worse than he'd suspected if the prospect of dredging up those memories was distasteful enough to dissuade her from setting her record straight. But unless she trusted him enough to share her traumatic history his hands were tied.

"It's possible the prosecuting attorney will find some evidence to link Stratton with your husband." Dale chose his words with care. "But he was skeptical. He couldn't understand why your husband would pay the sheriff to harass you. And I couldn't enlighten him. Without that background, I don't know that he'll put a priority on establishing that link. They already have enough evidence to prosecute Stratton and the 'clients' he's revealed. Since Barlow is dead, the state can't go after him anyway. Tying Stratton to Barlow will benefit you the most."

On impulse, he leaned across the table and entwined their fingers. She didn't even seem to notice. "This has to be your fight, Christine. And unless you're willing to talk about what happened, I'm not sure we'll get your record expunged. It will follow you for the rest of your life."

So much for small talk, Christine thought. Their casual ten-minute chat had taken a direction she'd never expected.

But he was right. When she'd left Dunlap, she'd hoped to put the past behind her. To start fresh. In the past few weeks, however, she'd come to realize that as long as her record was on the books, she would never be free of the nightmare.

Now Dale was offering her the possibility of erasing that record. And he believed her story without any proof. That, in itself, was a blessing that filled her with gratitude and endeared him to her in a way nothing else could have.

As she searched his kind, caring face, she was tempted to share with him the painful burden that had weighed down her heart for too long. And the irony of that wasn't lost on her. A few weeks ago, she would never have considered talking about her past with anyone, let alone a sheriff. But she'd come to respect this man. To believe that he was what he seemed to be—an honest and upright public official, a loving father, a man of integrity and honor.

It was his illness that had delivered the final blow to her defenses, she realized. In the past couple of days, as she'd watched him struggle with a debilitating infection, she'd relaxed around him. Weak and vulnerable, he'd seemed far less intimidating and threatening. And even though he was up and about again, she continued to feel safe with him.

Whether that would last once he regained full strength, she wasn't sure. But at this moment, sitting in his quiet kitchen, she was tempted to risk telling him her story. Yet she held back, knowing she could be making a big mistake, as she had once before. Fear coursed through her, leaving her uncertain.

Desperate for guidance, Christine found herself turning to God for the first time in years. Closing her eyes, she prayed in silence.

Lord, I know I haven't talked to You in a long while. My anger has been too great. But I've been doing a lot of thinking about Reverend Andrews's comment, and I suspect he may be right. That all the times I prayed to You, You were listening after all. And that it was Your grace that allowed me to endure.

I still don't understand why the nightmare had to happen, but I do know I've missed feeling Your presence in my life. I want to try and be open to that again. Please guide me now as I decide whether to share my story with Dale.

She felt a gentle squeeze on her hand and looked down in surprise to find her fingers entwined with Dale's. When had that happened? But she didn't pull away. His firm, supportive grip gave her the courage to consider taking a leap of faith. Far from being threatened by his strength, she felt protected—and safe. That was an illusion, of course. Yet it was one she didn't want to give up quite yet.

"It's a long story, Dale."

"I'm not going anywhere."

"Funny." A mirthless smile whispered at her lips. "I never thought I'd be willing to talk about this to anyone. Especially a sheriff."

Reaching over, he brushed her hair back from her face, his fingers lingering on her cheek, his touch as light as a drifting autumn leaf. "I'm not a sheriff today, Christine. I'm just a man. Who happens to care very much about helping a special woman clear up her past so she can truly make a fresh start."

As he stroked her cheek, the breath caught in her throat. But it was his soft words and tender tone that touched her heart.

And putting her trust in the Lord, she made her decision.

Chapter Twelve

As Christine stared into the black depths of her coffee, she realized she hadn't added any cream nor taken a sip. It was just as well. The last thing she needed was caffeine. Her heart was already pounding.

Pushing the mug aside, she balled her fingers into a fist and dropped her hand to her lap, leaving her other hand enfolded in Dale's comforting clasp.

"I don't even know where to start." Her voice was low and shaky.

"Why don't you tell me how you met your husband?" Dale had conducted enough interviews in the line of duty to know that backing up to a less volatile period often helped people ease into a recitation of the more traumatic events.

Following his suggestion, Christine filled him in on their meeting at the dinner, their whirlwind courtship and Jack's proposal.

"He was charming and attentive, and I was swept

off my feet. My mom liked him, too, and she was pretty particular. I think Jack's dad felt the same way about me, when Jack flew me to Dunlap to meet him." A tiny smile lifted the corners of her lips. "I liked his dad a lot. He ran the company with an iron fist, but he always struck me as a fair man. And he was very kind to me. His relationship with Jack, however, was always a bit rocky. He expected a lot from him, and Jack often didn't live up to those expectations.

"Anyway, things were okay for the first three years we were married. But it was never…" She stopped, as if searching for the right word, settling for what Dale figured was a gross understatement. "It wasn't what I'd hope it would be. And after the initial attraction subsided, there wasn't much else to sustain the marriage. Jack traveled more and more, and when he was in town he spent a lot of hours at the office. Even his father, who was very business focused, talked to Jack about his inattentiveness, but nothing changed. I'd hoped that once we started a family he might be home more, but I…I had two miscarriages, and…it seemed we weren't meant to have children."

A flash of regret and pain echoed in Christine's eyes, and Dale squeezed her hand. He'd seen her with Jenna and the children at story hour, watched how they gravitated to her, recalled the soft light that illuminated her face as she talked with them, and knew she would have made a great mother. The lack of children in her life had to be a great sorrow.

She confirmed his conclusion with her next comment. "Those were sad times for me. But I was also preoccupied with my mother. She was diagnosed with Alzheimer's soon after Jack and I married, and the disease progressed with incredible speed. Within a couple of years she needed around-the-clock professional care. There was a great facility near Dunlap, and Jack arranged for her to move there. It was expensive, but he never complained. I was grateful for his generosity, until I found out it came at a…price." She faltered, blinking back tears.

"Take your time, Christine." Dale cocooned her hand between both of his.

"I don't know if I can do this." With her free hand, she massaged her temple where a dull pain had begun to pound.

"Yes, you can. You owe it to yourself to get this out in the open so it can be addressed. Otherwise, your husband and Stratton will win."

"It's just that what happened is almost…surreal. Like a nightmare where you wake up and find yourself trapped in a room without windows or doors that keeps getting smaller and smaller. It's so bizarre that most people wouldn't believe me."

"I believe you." Dale stroked her cheek again. "Remember, I was a cop in L.A. for more than a decade. I saw the dregs of humanity. You can't tell me anything I haven't heard before." He ran his fingers across her temples in a featherlight touch. "Would some aspirin help?"

Touched by his sensitivity, she nodded. "Make it four."

"That's a lot."

"Trust me. I know what it takes to control these headaches."

Two minutes later, after she'd swallowed the aspirin in one gulp and he'd taken her hand again, she managed a rueful smile. "It's not too late to back out. I wouldn't blame you if you did."

He shook his head resolutely. "I'm in for the duration."

"Okay. But remember I warned you." She drew a steadying breath. "Things weren't perfect, but life was tolerable until Jack's father died of a heart attack not quite three years after we were married. A few weeks later, I overheard a rumor that Jack's absences might not be all business related. When I brought it up, something in him seemed to snap."

Christine swallowed, trying to summon up the courage to continue. Keeping her eyes downcast, she relayed the events of that horrible evening: Jack dragging her to the bedroom; Jack shoving her into the closet; her call to the police; Jack's implications to the sheriff that she drank; and his devastating revelation about why he'd married her.

When Christine finished, a heavy silence hung in the room while Dale tried to digest her story. He'd told her he'd seen it all. And he had. He'd responded to plenty of domestic violence cases. He'd run across countless cheating spouses. He'd dealt with his share of sadistic abusers.

But this was different.

This time he had a personal interest in the case.

As he thought about what Christine had endured, his typical detached compassion went out the window. Jack Barlow had brutally attacked his wife, then used her claustrophobia as a weapon against her. He'd paid off the police to ignore her plea for help, and capped the evening with the shocking news that he'd never loved her and that their marriage had always been a sham. Yet he'd told her he needed her to play the part of a devoted wife in public, for image reasons.

Despite Dale's solid belief in the tenet of his faith that instructed him to love his enemies, he found it hard to do anything but despise the man. Forgiveness wasn't even conceivable at this point.

Scooting his chair beside Christine's, Dale drew her into the circle of his arms. She was trembling badly, and he saw a silent tear plop onto the table.

"Sorry." She swiped at the moisture on her cheeks. "I thought I'd finished crying about this months ago." Her words were as shaky as the wet, frightened puppy he'd once rescued from the depths of a sewer drain.

"I don't know if there are enough tears to cover what you went through." He pressed his lips to her hair as a sudden protective urge swept over him, reinforcing his commitment to seeing justice done for the hurts she'd endured.

But first, he needed some answers. Christine struck him as an independent woman. She'd had no problem standing up to him when he'd gotten sick, and she'd been prepared to defend herself the night of the accident, despite her injury. There had to be a reason she hadn't walked out once Jack revealed his true character.

"Why didn't you leave, Christine?" The question was gentle, and he stroked his thumb over the back of her hand in a reassuring cadence.

"I wanted to. I even packed. But then Jack played his trump card."

A frown creased his brow. "His trump card?"

"My mother. She continued to deteriorate, and the cost of her care was escalating each month, into the five-figure range. Jack said that if I left, I'd get nothing. I knew he had friends in high places, and power, and I didn't doubt his ability to cut me off. Without his resources, there was no way I could afford to get my mother the kind of care I wanted her to have. And he knew how much I loved her."

His mind whirling, Dale tried to process the fact that Jack Barlow had blackmailed his own wife, using her love for her mother to tie her to him. For twelve long months, until he was killed in the plane crash, she'd had to endure his abuse. And a sadistic person like Barlow wasn't likely to pass up a chance to wield the power he held. What other horrors had the final year of her marriage held for Christine?

As if she'd read his mind, she spoke again. Her tone was tentative, as if she were testing the waters, seeing if he'd had enough. "There's more."

"I figured there was." His jaw tightened. "I'd like to hear it all."

With an almost imperceptible nod, she settled into the circle of his arms and picked up the story. "Jack never struck me or caused any serious physical damage. And most days, he left me alone. I knew he had other female…diversions. He only needed me to appear with him in public. I could have lived with the situation, if that's what it took to ensure my mom got the care she needed for the time she had left.

"Except Jack began to enjoy making my life miserable. Once, not long after that first blowup, he spiked my soft drink with something at a charitable event we attended. I got dizzy and began to slur my words. Everyone there—including the sheriff—thought I was drunk. It was a very clever way to establish public proof of my 'drinking problem.'" There was a bitter edge to her words, and she swallowed, trying to rid her mouth of the sour taste before she went on.

"After that, the sheriff started to harass me. Whenever I ventured out, he was on my tail. I got tickets for all kinds of alleged violations—speeding, running lights, parking. The worse was the DUI. I agreed to the breathalyzer because I knew it would come out fine, but he claimed it showed I was intoxicated. When he said I needed to come to his office, I resisted. The next thing I knew I was handcuffed and sitting in the patrol car. I'm sure he called Jack, who must have told him to give me the full treatment. Including the…the strip search." Even now, she found it difficult to say the words, difficult to swallow past the shame and humiliation.

"Did he do anything else to you, Christine?" Dale's voice was low and threaded with leashed anger.

"No." She knew what he meant, and she shook her head. "But I spent a sleepless night in a cell wondering if he would. When Jack came to get me the next day, the sheriff kept my license. Between the two of them, they managed to get it revoked for six months. We lived out in the country, meaning I was marooned. The only place Jack let me go was to visit my mother. Under the watchful eye of the driver he hired."

Dropping her volume a bit, she wadded her paper napkin into a tight ball. "In the end, it became a game with him. A sport, almost. He liked having power over me. I used to dread the days he was home with nothing to do, because that's when things got…really bad." The catch in her words was telling.

"How bad?" Again, Dale spoke in a low, controlled voice that sent a shiver up her spine.

"Pretty bad. He'd come looking for me, citing that passage from Paul about wives needing to submit to their husbands. I knew his sole purpose was to humiliate me, that he found perverse pleasure in my distress. I didn't want to give him that satisfaction, so I started letting him have his way without resisting. Once I did that, though, the game was boring and he turned to other ways of tormenting me."

"He used the claustrophobia."

"Yes. And I couldn't control my reaction to that."

"How often did he lock you in that closet, Christine?"

"Not often. But enough to keep me always on edge."

"For how long?"

"An hour the first time." Her volume dropped with each response.

"What about the worst time?"

Her reply came out in a whisper. "Fourteen hours."

Shock rippled through Dale. He'd seen how she'd reacted to a few minutes of imprisonment in the dark shed. An hour would have been torture. He couldn't begin to imagine how she'd survived fourteen.

"It was after I went to a neighboring town to try and arrange a loan to cover my mom's expenses. I figured if I could get enough funding for a year, I could leave Jack. My mom wasn't expected to live any longer than that. But I hadn't worked since my marriage, because I got pregnant almost right away and had a number of related health problems. I had no collateral. Everything was in Jack's name. And I had a police record. Anyway, Jack found out and…"

Bile rose in her throat, threatening to choke her. She

struggled to swallow past it, tightening her grip on Dale's hand.

"Take some slow, deep breaths, Christine." He touched her cheek, her hair, trying to erase the anguish from her face. He'd heard enough to plead her case to the prosecuting attorney. More than enough. "We can stop if you need to."

She focused on Dale's gentle instruction, breathing in and out, in and out, in a steady rhythm. "No. I want to finish."

A minute later, she resumed her story. "He went to w-work and didn't remember he'd locked me in the closet u-until he got home that night and started looking f-for me." Her words were choppy, the remembered horror squeezing the air from her lungs. "By then I—I couldn't stand, let alone walk. I was in such bad shape even he got scared."

For weeks, Dale had wondered what had happened to Christine to plant such deep hurt and wariness in her eyes. Now that he knew, he almost wished he didn't. The betrayal she'd endured at the hands of a man who had professed to love her was appalling. No one could go through an experience like that unscathed. That she'd not only endured but gone on to build a new life was a tribute to her strength.

Except she didn't look strong right now. Her head was bowed, her shoulders sagging in a posture of defeat. But she'd come too far, survived too much, not to see this fight through to the end.

Pushing prudence aside, Dale rose and pulled her to her feet. Wrapping his arms around her, he tucked her head against his chest and rested his cheek against her hair.

To his surprise, Christine didn't fight him or try to pull away. Instead, after stiffening for a brief moment, she relaxed in his arms, her body melting against his. He stroked her back, burying his face in her hair, inhaling the spicy scent that was uniquely hers as he thought of all she'd endured. Now he understood why she kept her distance from people, why her trust level was at such a low ebb. She'd been abused and humiliated and made to feel worthless by the very people who should have supported and defended her. More than anything, Dale wanted to reassure her that their behavior reflected *their* character, not hers. That whatever hurts she nursed in her heart, whatever blows her ego and esteem had sustained, she could overcome them. That any lingering doubts and insecurities from her traumatic experience didn't have to plague her for the rest of her life.

But he'd felt the same way about Linda, he acknowledged, and he'd failed to convince her of those same things. Her damage had been too severe, her scars too deep. Even his devoted love hadn't been able to help her overcome her shattered self-image, her bouts of depression, her bulimia. And if he hadn't been able to help his wife, there was little chance he could help Christine. The best he could hope to do for her was clear her name, allowing her to start over with a clean slate at least in legal terms.

Backing up a bit, he kept his arms looped around her. She looked up at him, searching his face, her vulnerable expression tugging at his heart.

"I think you got more than you bargained for," she whispered.

"I suspected some kind of abuse all along. But I had no idea about its extent. How did you keep going, day after day?"

"In the beginning, I prayed. But when God didn't respond, I took refuge in reading and gardening. They were my escape. And I knew my mother wasn't going to live very long. I figured I could survive. Still, by the end, I was…" She swallowed, struggling with the admission. "I was wishing God would hurry up and take her, as awful as that sounds." The words came out choked. "Then Jack's unexpected death gave me an early reprieve. The only emotion I felt when he died was relief."

"After all you'd been through, I think that was a normal reaction. My wife felt the same way about her stepfather." At her curious look, he explained. "Linda was abused by him as a child. She would never talk much about it, but I know the abuse continued until he died when she was fourteen. She told me once that instead of mourning, she celebrated that day. That she felt as if she'd finally been set free. But in the end, she couldn't escape his legacy. It colored the rest of her life and was manifested in many ways, including bulimia."

Sympathy suffused her face. "That must have been very hard for you."

Emotion tightened Dale's throat as he looked into Christine's warm, caring eyes. Her ability to put aside the trauma of her own story and focus on his difficulties was yet more evidence of her unselfishness and empathy.

"We had our challenges," he acknowledged. "But today isn't about me. It's about you. And getting your name cleared. After hearing your story, I'm more convinced than ever that your record needs to be erased."

"Stratton will never admit to any involvement with Jack."

"Your testimony could be powerful."

"It would be my word against his. He may not be credible, but I don't think anything I say would stand up in court without some hard evidence to back it up."

"The prosecuting attorney is looking for that now."

Dejected, she shook her head. "As you pointed out earlier, there's not a lot of incentive for him to put much effort into the search. Jack's dead. It sounds like they already have a case against Stratton. They won't waste their time just to clear my name."

"It's not a waste of time. It's pursuing justice. And I don't intend to ease off until every stone has been overturned."

She searched his face. "Is putting things right really that important to you?"

"Yes." He responded without hesitation, confining his answer to that single word. There was more he could say. Like, *you're important to me, too*. But he didn't want to lead her on. She'd been used enough by men who should have been doing their best to protect her. The last thing she needed was a man who professed feelings he couldn't follow up on. A man who was afraid to take the risk that loving Christine would entail.

Calling on every ounce of his willpower, he stepped back and let his arms drop to his sides. "I think I'll take your advice after all and lie down for a while."

Somehow she managed a forced smile. "I guess I wore you out. It might have been better to do this in installments. Like the daily soap operas on television, dishing out the melodrama in small doses."

Her ability to joke about her sordid story astounded him. Humor had never been a tool Linda could apply to her childhood trauma. Nor had his wife ever trusted Dale enough to share the kind of details Christine had revealed. He'd tried not to take it as a personal affront. Tried to remind himself that the scars she bore often kept her from sharing the secrets of her heart. Nevertheless, her withdrawal and holding back had been difficult to accept. And it had hurt their relationship.

It didn't appear that Christine had those issues.

Though she'd been wary when they'd met, once he'd proven himself trustworthy she'd been able to get past her prejudices and see him for himself, not as the reflection of a stereotype. Linda had never been able to do that.

The differences between the two women resonated with Dale. Made him question his decision to keep his distance from Christine. But today wasn't the time to think this through. Later, after he felt stronger, he'd revisit the situation. And in the meantime, he wasn't about to burn any bridges with this special woman.

"I appreciate your trust, Christine." He touched her cheek once again. "We'll talk more about next steps as soon as I feel better."

As Christine watched him disappear down the hall, she wondered if his comment about next steps had been in reference to her fight to clear her name or to their relationship. Because they did have a relationship, much to her surprise. How it had developed, she had no idea. Nor did she have any idea where it was headed. She was even less sure where she *wanted* it to head.

Confused, she sat back down at the kitchen table and reached for her mug. But when she lifted it to her lips, she discovered that the coffee had grown as cold as her dreams of romance and a family.

Yet as she nuked it back to life, she saw another parallel. Like the coffee, her dreams were also being resurrected. By a small-town sheriff, of all people.

Thanks to Dale Lewis, she was rethinking her resolution to lead a solitary life.

There was much baggage still to deal with, of course. And she knew that many pitfalls and hurdles lay ahead. Perhaps too many to overcome.

But for the first time in years, an ember of hope sprang to life in her heart, filling it with warmth and optimism and a growing conviction that a brighter tomorrow might lie ahead.

Chapter Thirteen

"You ever heard the term 'two sheets to the wind'?"

As Dale shut the door to the sheriff's office behind him, he gave Marv a wry grin. "You're about as good for my ego as Christine."

"You wouldn't be referring to Christine Turner, would you?" Interest flared in the deputy's eyes. "The woman who shies away from uniforms?"

"That's the one." Dale headed for the coffeemaker, but changed his mind halfway there. He was pretty sure his stomach wasn't yet up to the high-octane stuff Marv brewed. "Anything going on?"

"You tell me." Marv folded his arms across his chest, his expression curious. "How'd you break through those walls she puts up?"

"My mom left her checkbook at the library last week, and Christine stopped by to drop it off." Dale continued toward the coffeemaker and rummaged through the cabinet underneath. "She caught me in the throes of salmonella and offered to watch Jenna over the weekend until I felt better. Do we have any tea?"

"Worried about the kid, huh? That makes sense. Women are soft touches with children. Nope, no tea. You must still be feeling poorly if you prefer that over coffee."

"Let's just say I'm being cautious."

"So what are you doing here, anyway? I thought you wanted me to fill in all day today and go to half days tomorrow?"

"I have some things I need to do this morning while Jenna's at preschool. And I'm going to take her to story hour at the library after lunch."

"The way you look, you should have stayed in bed."

"I needed a change of scene."

"Not much of a vacation for you, is it?"

"You've got that right." Dale had planned to drop Jenna at preschool every morning while his mother was away, instead of her normal three days a week, work in the mornings, then take half days of vacation in the afternoon to watch her. That schedule hadn't worked out yet, but he planned to implement it tomorrow. In the meantime, he wanted to brief the prosecuting attorney in Nebraska on the information Christine had shared with him.

"You sure you don't want to take a few more days off? I finished replacing the rose arbor, so Alice is off my case—until she comes up with another project. I have time to fill in."

"Thanks, but I'm improving. And according to Sam I should start feeling a whole lot better soon."

The man shrugged. "It's your body. You want me to run down to Gus's and get you a cup of tea?"

"I appreciate the offer, but I won't be here long enough to drink it."

"Anything I can help you with?" Marv settled back at his desk.

"No. I just want to run through my mail and make a quick call."

Closing his office door behind him, Dale moved toward his desk, giving his mail a cursory glance as he eased into his chair. Despite his comments to Marv, he was struggling with the aftereffects of the food poisoning. The exertion of getting Jenna ready for preschool, dropping her off and coming into the office had wiped him out. Christine had offered to stop by again, but he'd declined, unwilling to take advantage of her generosity. In fact, today he intended to try and repay some of it.

As he tapped in the number for the prosecuting attorney's office, he prayed that the man would be in. He'd have called yesterday if he'd felt up to it, but he'd spent all morning sleeping while Jenna was at preschool, and she'd required all his attention and energy in the afternoon. By the time he'd tucked her in at eight o'clock, he'd stumbled to his own room and fallen asleep sprawled across the bed with his clothes on. He hadn't moved a muscle until morning.

Relief surged through him when Andrew Briggs's secretary put the call through.

"Mr. Briggs? Dale Lewis."

"I'm glad you called, Sheriff. I have some interesting information to pass on." Dale heard papers being shuffled. "We did some checking into Jack Barlow's finances, and it appears that on a number of occasions he withdrew funds from the ATM machine in five-hundred and thousand-dollar increments on the same day, or within a day or two, that Stratton made deposits in the same amounts."

"Stratton could deny any connection."

"True. But we also discovered that the former owner of his current car was Barlow. And it doesn't appear any money changed hands in that transaction."

Circumstantial evidence, but telling nonetheless, Dale reflected. And coupled with Christine's story, it could be incriminating.

"I have some news for you, too." Dale related Christine's story, including her witnessing the first payoff, with as much professional detachment as possible. "The question is, where do we go from here?"

"As I understand it, your primary interest is seeing that Ms. Turner's record is expunged, is that correct?"

"Yes, and also that justice is done. The Strattons of the world give all cops a bad name."

"Trust me, I'm working very hard to ensure he pays for what he's done. If I have my way, he'll serve a good chunk of time despite the plea bargain. As for

Ms. Turner's record, the easiest way to accomplish that is for Stratton to admit Barlow was paying him off for the harassment. And I think I'm armed with enough material to make Stratton squirm. Can you get a written statement from Ms. Turner?"

"No problem."

"Send it to me as soon as possible, and with that in hand, plus the additional evidence we've uncovered, we'll confront Stratton. My guess is he'll confess. He put up a pretty tough front at first, but the more we've uncovered, the more cooperative he's become. Once we have an admission of complicity, expunging Ms. Turner's record shouldn't be a problem."

"You'll keep me informed?"

"Of course."

Severing the connection, Dale flipped the switch on his computer. As he waited for it to warm up so he could prepare a statement for Christine to review and sign, he said a silent prayer of thanks. Gary Stratton might think his dealings with Barlow were as dead as the man himself, but he was about to discover otherwise. If everything worked as it should, justice would be done.

As for Barlow, Dale wished he, too, would have been forced to pay the price for what he'd done to Christine. But in death, his fate had been handed over to a higher power—a God who was forgiving…but also just. And Dale trusted the Lord to deal with Stratton as the man deserved.

* * *

When Dale and Jenna walked into the library as Christine opened the book to begin her first story, her eyes widened in surprise. She'd expected Dale to spend every spare minute resting—and by the look of him, that's what he should be doing. His cheeks still had an unnatural pallor, and there were lines of weariness at the corners of his eyes.

Despite the aftereffects of his illness, however, he radiated a natural virility that tripped her pulse into double time. Dressed in jeans, an open-necked, dark blue cotton shirt and a black leather jacket, he didn't look anything like a cop today.

"Hi, Ms. Christine!" Jenna waved and trotted across the room, settling into a cross-legged position in the circle of children on the floor.

"Hello, Jenna. I'm glad you could come." She glanced toward Dale, and he smiled and lifted a hand in greeting. Standing near the wall, one shoulder propped against some shelving, he looked ready to drop. "There are chairs and magazines on the other side for anyone who'd like to take a break while we read stories." Christine's gaze swept over the adults who were standing around in the back, ending with Dale. He gave a slight nod, pushed off from the wall and wandered to the far side of the room.

An hour later, when Christine went to retrieve the treat of the day from behind the front desk, she scanned the chairs in the reading area. Dale had chosen a spot in the corner, and a magazine lay in his lap. But his head was tipped back against the wall, and from his even breathing and the slack lines of his mouth she knew he was asleep.

A rush of tenderness swept over her as she traced his strong profile, softened now in slumber. Despite his illness, he'd brought Jenna to the story hour she awaited with such eagerness. He was a good dad. Not to mention a good man.

"What kind of cookies do we have today, Ms. Christine?"

Forcing herself to look away from Dale, Christine smiled down at one of her story hour regulars. "Sugar cookies. Would you like to take them over to the other boys and girls?"

Pleased to be charged with such an important duty, the little boy smiled. "Okay. I'll pass them around, like you do."

"Thank you very much, Justin. I'll be over in a minute or two."

She waited until the children were clustered around the plate of cookies before moving toward Dale. Up close, the lines of exhaustion in his face were more pronounced, the shadows under his eyes silent testimony to his ordeal. His hair, always neatly combed, was in slight disarray, and she was tempted to brush it back from his forehead.

Without making a conscious decision, she reached out to him, but his eyelids flickered and she retracted her arm, feeling like a kid caught with her hand in the cookie jar.

Straightening up, he gave her a lopsided grin. "I must have dozed off."

"You look like you needed the rest."

He shook his head. "Between you and Marv, there won't be much left of my ego."

"You went to the office today?"

"For a few minutes. I had some business I needed to take care of." He stood and lowered his voice. "Is there somewhere we can talk in private for a few minutes?"

"There's an office in the back, but I'm the only one here and I can't…"

"My word, Dale! Marv was right. You look awful!"

Turning in unison toward the front door, they watched as Marge barreled toward them, her calf-length leopard-print coat flapping about her legs.

"Hello, Marge." Dale gave her an amused smile. "I'll have to be sure and thank my deputy for passing that opinion on."

"Now don't you hold it against him. Sam told me the same thing. As did half a dozen other people I ran into this morning. I can't believe I just found out about this today. Goodness, I would have brought over some casseroles and offered to babysit Jenna if I'd known."

"Ms. Christine came to our house. She cooked me dinner and we watched movies and she took good care of my daddy." All heads swiveled toward Jenna as she joined them. "These are good cookies, Ms. Christine. Justin wants to know if we can each have two."

"Yes, there should be enough."

When Christine looked back at Marge, the woman's speculative expression brought a flush to her cheeks.

"That was very neighborly of you, my dear. I'm sure Jenna and Dale appreciated your help very much."

Unsure how to respond, Christine looked at Dale, who seemed unperturbed by the woman's obvious interest.

"She was a godsend," Dale confirmed. "I was knocked flat. Trust me, I will never again eat food that has been unrefrigerated for more than half an hour." Folding his arms across his chest, Dale gave Marge his most winning smile. "Speaking of favors, I wonder if I could impose on you. I need to speak in private to Christine, and she doesn't want to leave the front desk unattended. Do you think you could keep an eye on things in general and Jenna in particular for ten minutes while we talk in the back office?"

"Why, I'd be happy to. You two take your time. I might even help myself to a cookie or two, if there are any left."

"Thanks, Marge." Taking Christine's arm, Dale nudged her toward the back of the library.

She waited until they were out of earshot to speak. "This isn't a great idea. You're adding fuel to the fire."

"What do you mean?" He kept moving, heading toward the door marked Private.

"Did you see how she was looking at us? Like she thought there was…that we were…" Her voice trailed off. "Anyway, she looked…curious."

"About us?" Dale pushed open the door and guided her inside, closing it behind them. "Don't worry about it. Marge is curious about everything. And she's a closet romantic. She's always looking to pair people up." He settled one hip on the edge of the desk, motioning Christine into a chair across from him. "I have some news from Dunlap."

Concerns about Marge vanishing, Christine sank into the chair. She listened in silence as Dale explained the close timing of the withdrawals and deposits in Stratton's and Barlow's accounts, as well as the car title discovery.

"Add in your eyewitness account of a money exchange, and Andrew Briggs, the prosecuting attorney, thinks he has enough to confront Stratton," Dale concluded.

Trying to temper the hope that flared within her, Christine leaned forward. "What does that mean for me?"

"If he can get Stratton to admit that your husband paid him off to harass you and falsify records, Briggs doesn't think we'll have much problem getting your record wiped clean."

"And if he doesn't admit it?"

"Briggs thinks he will. He says the more evidence they've uncovered, the more cooperative Stratton has become. But he does need a written statement from you before he confronts Stratton." Dale withdrew several folded sheets of paper from the inside pocket of his jacket and held them out to her. "I put this together based on what you told me. Considering how I felt that day, it's possible I've misrepresented some things, so feel free to make any necessary corrections. Once it's finalized, signed and witnessed, I'll fax a copy to Briggs and over-night the original."

Christine took the papers but her focus remained on Dale. "This is why you went to the office this morning?"

"I didn't want to lose any time."

His face blurred as tears welled in Christine's eyes. Despite his illness, Dale had gone to great effort on her behalf. Gratitude—and something more—filled her heart.

"Hey, it's going to be okay, Christine." Dale entwined his fingers with hers and spoke in a husky voice. "I can't change the past, but I'm going to do my best to help you have a better future."

"I don't know what to say." She choked out the words. "Thank you doesn't seem close to adequate."

"We're not home-free yet," he cautioned. "Save your thanks for the day we get word that your record has been cleared."

"No." She looked up at him intently. "My thanks

have nothing to do with whether or not we succeed. They're for… everything you've done to show me that not all cops are bad and not all men are jerks."

With a gentle finger he brushed away the tear that was following the delicate curve of her jaw toward her chin. "There are some good guys still around."

"I think I was lucky to cross paths with one of the best." Her comment came out in a whisper.

His eyes darkened, and Christine heard the breath catch in his throat. He wanted to kiss her. She could read it on his face as clearly as if he'd spoken the words. And despite all her well-laid plans for a solitary life, she wanted him to.

Fear held her back, however. Like a government warning label, a red flag appeared in her mind, bearing a cautionary message: loving carries risk. It was a truth she knew all too well. Just as she knew that taking risks required courage—and trust. Much to her regret, she didn't know if she had an adequate supply of either to pursue the attraction that sizzled between her and the sheriff.

But she wasn't alone in her doubts, Christine realized. As she looked at Dale, she saw her own conflict reflected in his eyes. And how could she blame him? She came with lots of baggage. Few men would want to take on a woman with such a sordid past. Especially a man who'd already had a problem-plagued wife.

Tears once more pricked her eyelids, this time

prompted by disappointment, and a sense of loss. But she blinked them back and stood, extricating her hand from his as she took a step back. "I'll read this as soon as I get home and return it to you by tomorrow, if that's okay."

"That will be fine." He rose, too.

"I need to relieve Marge." She edged toward the door.

"I know." He held her gaze captive for a moment, his expression troubled. "Christine, I think we need to…"

"I have to get out there." She fumbled for the knob. "I'll talk to you tomorrow."

Slipping out the door, she drew a deep, steadying breath. She had to pull herself together or she'd risk feeding Marge's curiosity about what was going on between the town sheriff and the organic farmer.

And since there wasn't anything at all going on—nor was there likely to be, given that look in Dale's eyes—Christine didn't want rumors floating around Oak Hill. She needed to play it calm and cool on the outside…even if she felt the exact opposite on the inside.

Chapter Fourteen

Balancing the phone against her shoulder, Christine listened as Dale's home answering machine kicked in. She'd hoped he was taking it easy while Jenna was at preschool, but he must have gone into work—again. This time not on her account, she hoped.

Her second attempt to reach him, at the office, succeeded. He answered the phone in his "official" voice, but warmth softened it when she greeted him. Or was she imagining things? she wondered, as she inquired how he was feeling.

"Much better. I ate a regular dinner last night. And it stayed down."

"I'm glad to hear that." She sat on the stool at her kitchen island and played with the edge of the papers he'd handed her yesterday. She'd read the statement he'd put together—and also read between the lines. Although it was a professional presentation, the clipped style and cut-no-slack tone reflected the hostility he felt toward the men who had mistreated her.

But she couldn't argue with the facts he'd set down. He'd captured her story dead-on. With just a couple of minor edits, she was ready to sign it. "I finished reviewing the statement. I can drop it off at your office this morning, if that's okay."

"I have a better idea. You have a fax machine, don't you?"

"Yes."

"Send it to me. I'll make any changes you've noted and bring it out for you to sign after I pick up Jenna from preschool at noon."

"I don't want to put you to any trouble."

"It's no trouble, Christine. Besides, Jenna misses seeing you around the house." And so did he. But he kept that thought to himself.

"If you're sure…thanks, that would be great."

Three hours later, when the crunch of gravel on her drive announced their arrival, Christine wiped her palms on her jeans and headed toward the front door, willing the flutter in the pit of her stomach to settle down. Dale was coming on official business, she reminded herself. Besides, Jenna was with him. The youngster's presence was sure to keep things light and impersonal. There was nothing to be nervous about.

At least there wasn't until Christine pulled open the front door and watched as Dale released Jenna from her safety harness, then reached farther into the car and withdrew a wicker picnic hamper.

"Hi, Ms. Christine!" Jenna ran up the walk toward the porch while Dale followed at a more sedate pace.

"Hi, honey." She bent to give the little girl a hug, but her focus was on Dale and the picnic hamper. "What's that for?"

He grinned. "It's lunchtime, isn't it? And I have a lot of eating to catch up on. Jenna and I decided an indoor picnic might be fun, and we hoped you'd join us. If you have the table, we have the food."

"We brought brownies," Jenna offered. "And soup. I told Daddy you weren't supposed to have soup on a picnic, but he said it was okay in November."

The soup must be a concession to the delicate condition of Dale's stomach, Christine surmised. Folding her arms, she inspected the hamper. "I think I can supply the table. Provided the food isn't from Gus's."

"Perish the thought!" Dale gave her a look of mock horror. "I called Cara to ask if she could prepare a gourmet picnic, and voilà." He held up the basket. "I don't know what's inside, other than the brownies and soup. But it smells great. And I've eaten her food at the inn. Trust me, you won't be disappointed."

"I'm sold." She stepped aside and gestured toward the door. "Come on in."

With Jenna trotting at his heels, Dale headed toward the kitchen. He set the basket on the counter and turned to Christine, withdrawing several sheets of paper from a small portfolio he'd tucked under his arm. "The revisions. Why don't you look them over in the living room while Jenna and I set out the food. If you don't mind letting me use your fax machine, I'd like to send a signed copy to Andrew Briggs as soon as possible. I'll witness your signature whenever you're ready."

Ten minutes later, when Christine re-entered the kitchen, a veritable feast covered the checkered cloth that had been spread on her kitchen table. A hearty beef barley soup, crusty French bread, chilled poached chicken breasts in a raspberry sauce and various side dishes—not to mention the promised brownies—filled the surface. And there were peanut butter and jelly sandwiches for Jenna, cut into animal shapes.

"Wow! This isn't like any picnic I've ever been on." Christine moved to the counter and picked up a pen.

"Cara's a wonder in the kitchen." Dale set a glass of water on the table and joined her. "Everything okay now?"

"Yes. All the changes are perfect. And the write-up is very thorough. You were so sick, I wasn't sure you absorbed half of what I told you."

"I heard every word, Christine." His quiet but intense response left no room for doubt.

Leaning down to hide the flush on her cheeks, she signed the document and handed the pen to Dale, watching as he added his signature in a few bold strokes.

"My office is off the kitchen." She indicated a doorway. "The fax machine is on the side table."

"I'll be right back. You and Jenna go ahead and fix your plates."

The fax went through without any glitches, and Dale rejoined them within a couple of minutes, tucking the original document into the portfolio as he surveyed the table. Christine and Jenna's plates were filled, their soup bowls brimming. Propping his hands on his hips, he gave them a teasing grin. "You ladies didn't waste any time, did you?"

"But we didn't start yet, Daddy. We waited for you to say a blessing."

As he took his seat, he sent Christine a questioning look. "Do you mind?"

"No. I always used to pray before meals, until… anyway, I'm trying to mend that relationship. Reminders like this help."

"Good for you." He reached for her hand and squeezed it. Taking Jenna's hand as well, Dale bowed his head. "We thank you, Lord, for this special meal and for allowing us to share it together. We ask you to bless this food, and we pray that Your healing grace will fill our lives. Help us feel Your presence and know You are always near, and guide our steps when we stumble. Thank you for my quick recovery, and for those who helped bring it about. Amen."

An hour later, after a relaxed, laughter-filled meal, Christine smiled and shook her head as she inspected their plates. "I'd say we did Cara's handiwork justice. Especially you." She raised one eyebrow as she looked at Dale.

"Hey, I had six days to catch up on."

"You didn't have to do it all in one sitting."

"Are you implying I overate?"

"If the shoe fits…" She lifted one shoulder. "I only hope you don't regret this."

"I'll be fine. I can see the improvement almost hour by hour."

In truth, he did seem much better. Since his visit to the library yesterday, his face had regained most of its color and the fine lines around his eyes had eased.

"It's too bad your mother was gone. She could have helped a lot."

He smiled at her. "I had a good substitute."

"Ms. Christine, can I go look at your garden?"

Grateful for Jenna's interruption, Christine transferred her attention to the little girl. "There's not much left to see this late in the fall, honey."

"There were some pretty flowers on the side of the house."

Jenna must have noticed the few hardier annuals that hadn't yet succumbed to frost, Christine speculated. "We can go out and look. Would you like to take a bouquet home?"

"May I?"

"You two go ahead. I'll clean up." Dale rose and began collecting the empty containers.

"We'll only be a few minutes." Taking Jenna's hand, Christine grabbed a pair of scissors from a kitchen drawer.

"No hurry. I have the afternoons off until my mom gets back next Friday."

By the time they returned with a gigantic bouquet, Dale had everything stowed in the wicker hamper. Christine wrapped the flowers in newspaper and followed the pair out to the car, a book tucked under her arm.

Once Dale had Jenna strapped in, Christine leaned in and placed the flowers next to the little girl, handing her the book. "We just got this at the library, and I wanted you to be the first one to check it out. I was going to give it to your daddy when I saw him, but I'm glad I got to give it to you myself."

A smile lit Jenna's face as she looked at the colorful cover illustration of two children in a magical garden. "I'll ask Daddy to read it to me when we get home. Thank you, Ms. Christine."

"You're welcome, honey. You can look at the pictures while I say goodbye to your daddy."

Straightening up, Christine closed the door. Dale had stowed the wicker hamper in the trunk, and she joined him at the back of the car. "I enjoyed the impromptu picnic. Thank you for including me."

"It was small repayment for all you did for us this past week."

"You have it backward. I was the one who owed you a favor."

Now that he'd heard her story, Dale understood her reluctance to be indebted to anyone. But he wanted her to understand that not everyone had a hidden agenda for their kindness. "I was glad to help, Christine. And like the Good Samaritan, I didn't expect anything in return. That's not what Christian charity is all about."

"Too bad Jack didn't feel the same way." A twinge of pain tightened her features, and she shivered in her short-sleeved blouse as a sudden gust of cold wind whipped past.

Without stopping to think, Dale drew her close, rubbing the palms of his hands up and down her bare arms. "You should go inside." His voice wasn't quite steady, and despite his suggestion, he didn't release her.

A tremor rippled through her as the friction warmed both her skin and her heart. And all at once she found it difficult to breathe. She was close enough to feel the heat from his body, she realized. Close enough to get lost in his blue eyes. Close enough to stretch on tiptoes and press her lips to his.

That last thought jolted her.

In light of the tender yearning on Dale's face, however, she suspected she wasn't the only one with romantic notions. A few days ago, when he'd told her that after he felt better they'd talk about next steps, she'd wondered if he was referring to the battle to clear her name or their relationship. Considering all he was doing to wipe her record off the books, she'd figured he meant the former.

Yet she didn't think she'd imagined the spark between them the night she'd stayed at his house, nor in the office at the library. And she didn't think she was imagining it now. Like her, however, he was walking a wide circle around it.

But Christine was growing tired of those evasive maneuvers. And beginning to think they were unnecessary—at least with this man. Dale had told her once that he was one of the good guys. While she'd been skeptical then, she wasn't any longer. And even though she was still scared, even though she wasn't sure she could trust her instincts, they were too powerful to ignore. Try as she might, she seemed unable to step back from his arms.

Dale was having the same difficulty. With Christine mere inches away, her skin smooth and silky beneath his fingertips, he couldn't ignore the message in her soft brown eyes. During most of their encounters, he'd seen distrust and caution in their depths. But now wariness had given way to welcome and warmth, and aversion had become invitation.

Self-discipline had always been one of Dale's strengths. But he couldn't muster it now as his gaze locked with Christine's and a powerful jolt of electricity sizzled between them. He didn't want to lead her on. But neither could he resist her silent entreaty or the wistful yearning that illuminated her face.

Warning bells went off in his mind, but Dale disregarded them. He'd been attracted to her for weeks. Had spent more than one lonely, wakeful night thinking about her, imagining an encounter like this, yet never dreaming she'd lower her defenses enough to allow him to get close. Now that she had, he didn't have the strength to walk away without tasting her lips.

Angling his body to shield Christine from Jenna's view, he swept her soft hair back from her face. She shivered again, but whether from cold or anticipation he couldn't tell. Never breaking eye contact, he signaled his intent by brushing his fingertips across her lips, watching for some sign that she wanted him to stop. When none came, when she swayed toward him instead, he gave up the fight. Lowering his lips to hers, he drank of her sweetness in a tender, caring—and careful—kiss. She deserved nothing less after the sadistic, brutal treatment she'd endured at the hands of her husband.

As Dale's lips moved over hers, gentle and almost reverent, Christine felt something deep inside her release, like the untwisting of a coiled spring. The sensation of relief, of an easing of pressure and tension, soothed and calmed her as nothing else had in years. She'd forgotten how good it could feel to trust another person, to believe in—and count on—someone. To feel secure enough to lose herself in the moment, confident that other person would keep her safe.

That was how she felt in Dale's arms. Safe. And cherished. And loved.

When he deepened the kiss, she didn't protest, giving even more than he asked for. Lost in the wonder of his arms, she wished the interlude could go on forever.

All too soon, however, he eased his lips away from hers, his lingering release making it clear he was no more anxious to end the embrace than she was. But Jenna was in the car, and this wasn't the time or place to explore what their kiss had begun.

He rested his forehead against hers, his breath warm on her cheeks. "I'll call you." He sounded as ragged as she felt.

"Okay." She could manage nothing more than a whisper.

Drawing back, he looked down at her, as if memorizing her features. She couldn't read his eyes, but she was sure her own offered a window to her soul.

At last Christine forced herself to step away. "Drive safe." The words came out in a breathless rush.

"I will." Lifting his hand, he touched her cheek once more. Then he slid into the car, disappearing a couple of minutes later in a cloud of dust.

For a long while, Christine remained outside, the warm glow in her heart a buffer against the cold wind. But at last, as Dale's absence lengthened, the chill seeped into her, bringing with it a bucketful of doubts. Had she been wrong to encourage him?

Should she have been more cautious, worked out her own issues before jumping into the fire? Were either of them ready to travel the path they'd started down?

Recalling Dale's comment about next steps, Christine knew she needed to think those through as well. She didn't want anyone to get hurt, including Jenna. It was important she do the right thing for everyone…except she didn't know what that was. She needed guidance, just as she had when life with Jack had become a nightmare.

In those days, the Lord hadn't seemed to respond to her pleas for counsel. Or perhaps she'd been listening for the answer she'd wanted rather than the answer He'd offered, as Reverend Andrews had suggested. If she went to Him now, with no preconceived notions and an open heart, maybe things would be different.

It was worth a try, anyway. Because she didn't know where else to turn.

As the last hymn of the Sunday service ended and the congregation began to file out, Christine took her seat again. She waved at Cara and Sam as they exited, and nodded to a few people she'd met on her first visit to the church. There was no sign of Dale and Jenna, and she was grateful for that. According to Jenna, they never missed a Sunday, but often came to the early service. That's why she'd chosen the later one.

Though Christine had been praying for guidance

since their impromptu picnic three days ago, she hadn't yet received it. She was hoping that here, in the Lord's house, His voice might be easier to discern.

Quiet descended as the last worshippers departed, and Christine settled her Bible on her lap and focused on the cross in the sanctuary.

Lord, I need Your help. After my nightmare with Jack, I never expected to face this dilemma because I didn't plan to let any man get close again. But Dale is very special. At least that's what my heart is telling me. Yet fear is distorting my perspective. I want to trust him, but my faith in my own judgment is shaky. I need Your wisdom, Lord, and Your courage. I can't seem to figure this out on my own. Please...show me what path I should take in order to live my life according to Your will.

Closing her eyes, Christine tried to put anxiety aside and place her trust in the Lord. After a while, as the peace and stillness of the church surrounded her, she felt the knot of tension in her stomach begin to relax. A welcome calmness settled over her, and though she heard no voice, she sensed a comforting, serene presence that seemed to wrap her in a loving embrace.

When she felt a gentle pressure on her shoulder, she responded slowly, reluctant to break the consoling connection. At last, however, she looked up to find Reverend Andrews standing beside her in the deserted church, a kind smile warming his face.

"I saw you during the service and hoped you'd join

us for the social hour. I inquired about you, and Marge said Cara had told her you'd stayed behind to pray. I hope I'm not intruding, but I wanted to make sure everything was all right."

The meditative mood was slipping away, much to her regret, but Christine was touched by the minister's concern. "I just needed to think for a while."

"You chose a good place. Take as long as you like."

He started to turn away, but Christine's next comment stopped him. "By the way, I heard from Erin. She's got a job and has enrolled in night school to get her GED. It sounds like she's on the road to building a new life."

"I had a note from her, too. It's not easy to start over, but your kindness was a great encouragement to her."

"I didn't do much."

"You did a great deal, Christine. You cared. You took her in when she was hurting. You put yourself at risk to give her shelter and support."

"She needed help. I couldn't turn my back."

"Many people would have."

She swallowed past the lump in her throat and looked down at her Bible. "Not if they'd walked in her shoes."

In the silence that followed her comment, Christine blinked back sudden tears. When at last she lifted her head, the compassion in the minister's eyes tightened her throat.

"May I?" He gestured toward the pew and, at her nod, sat beside her. "I sensed a connection between you and Erin that night at your house. I wondered if you might have personal knowledge of what she was going through."

"My situation wasn't an exact parallel, but I know what it's like to be trapped in a bad relationship, to feel alone and abandoned, with no one to help."

"Including God." It was a statement, not an accusation.

"Yes. I tried praying, Reverend. In the beginning I prayed for fortitude and courage. Later, I prayed for a way out."

"And you didn't think God heard your prayers?"

"No. And by the time I did get a reprieve, I'd lost my trust in His kindness and mercy."

"Yet you endured and went on to build a new life. Could you have done that without His help?"

"I've reflected on that since we had our first conversation, and I don't think so. I believe God's grace brought me to where I am. But I'm not sure I'll ever understand why He wanted me to go through all the pain. Nor do I understand why I stopped feeling His presence."

"Perhaps anger is the culprit for the latter. It can harden our hearts and create walls that shut other people—and God—out, even when they stand ready to help."

"I did have a lot of anger, but that's dissipated. And

I'm trying to re-establish my relationship with the Lord. I need His guidance on a problem I'm wrestling with, but I'm not getting any answers to my questions."

"Could it be the questions that are the problem?"

"I'm not sure I understand what you mean." She gave him a puzzled look.

A smile curved his mouth. "It's like the old game of twenty questions. Have you ever played it?"

"As a child. I seem to recall that you get twenty questions to identify some place or person or object."

"That's right. The trick is to make the best use of your questions. When I was a boy, my sister would drive me crazy, because she'd always ask questions that weren't pertinent. If we were trying to identify a person, for example, she always assumed it was a film star and asked questions related to movies. Most often, the person had no connection to Hollywood, so we wasted a lot of questions up front. God, of course, doesn't have a limit on the number of questions we can ask, but we can speed things up if we focus on the most pertinent ones."

Was that her problem? Christine wondered. Had she been asking the wrong questions? And could this man help her frame the right ones?

Wrapping her hands around her Bible, she looked at him. "May I speak with you in confidence?"

"Discretion is a minister's stock in trade," he

assured her with a smile. "I only share people's confidences with God."

A brief answering smile flashed across her face. "My problem has to do with Dale Lewis. He and I...well, over the past few weeks, we've..." She stopped, regrouped and started over. "The thing is, Reverend, I like him a lot. But I've had some very bad experiences with men in general, and sheriffs in particular, that have made me wary. Plus, I've made mistakes about people's character that have caused me to question my own judgment. As a result, I decided to steer clear of relationships. Then I met Dale."

When she stopped, the minister spoke. "And you fell in love."

"Yes." Hearing it put into words was a bit of a shock. But it was the truth.

"Does he feel the same way?"

"I think he's attracted to me, but he has issues, too. Do you know much about his marriage?"

"Some. He and I talked quite a bit after he came back to Oak Hill."

"In that case, you may know that his wife had problems that affected their relationship. I doubt Dale wants to saddle himself with another damaged woman."

"Do you think of yourself as damaged?"

She considered the question. "I was badly hurt. And I never expected to be able to trust a man again. But since I trust Dale, I suppose the scars aren't debilitating."

"He'll see that in time."

She hoped that was true. But it didn't solve her own problem. "I still have to address my issues with fear. I learned the hard way that behind closed doors, people aren't always what they seem in public."

"True. In the end we have to use our best judgment and trust our hearts."

"Those have failed me in the past."

"Then put it in God's hands."

"I've tried. I've asked Him what I should do, but I'm not hearing a response."

"That brings me back to the concept of asking the right questions." Reverend Andrews propped an elbow on the back of the pew and angled toward her. "Maybe instead of asking the Lord to tell you what you should do, you could ask him to help you ask the questions of *yourself* that will allow you to make a sound decision."

"I'm open to ideas about what those might be."

"Try these. Do you want to let fear win and live the rest of your life alone? Or are you willing to believe that Dale is who he appears to be, put your trust in the Lord and open your heart to love?"

With a start, Christine realized that in two brief questions the minister had homed in on her key issues.

All along, she supposed she had been waiting for God to make her decision for her. But as Reverend

Andrews had suggested, perhaps the best thing He could do for her was help her ask the important questions and give her discernment as she worked through the answers.

She knew one thing already: she'd had enough regrets in her life. Years down the road, she didn't want to look back and lament a lost opportunity to share her life with a special man and a little girl who had already claimed a place in her heart. Not if that was the path God wanted her to tread.

Reaching out, she clasped the minister's hand. "I can't thank you enough for your help, Reverend."

"I'm just the messenger, Christine." Once more, a smile tipped up his lips as he engulfed her fingers in a comforting clasp. "My boss is the one who deserves your thanks. He helps me find the words I need."

Rising, he inclined his head toward the Bible in her lap. "You might try Jeremiah 29, verses eleven to thirteen. I've always found that passage to be a comfort in times of uncertainty. And Marge wanted me to tell you she's saving you a cup of coffee and a chocolate donut, whenever you're finished here." With a wink and a wave, he stepped out of the pew.

As he headed toward the back of the church, Christine paged through the book to the verses he'd referenced.

For I know well the plans I have for you, says the Lord, plans for your welfare not for woe, plans to give you a future full of hope. When you call me, when you go to pray to me, I will listen to you. When you look for me, you will find me.

Closing the Bible, Christine drew a slow, deep breath. She'd come to church that morning unsettled and tense. While she still had a lot of thinking to do, at least she no longer felt so alone or lost. During her contemplative respite after the service, she'd found comfort in the stillness of the church, had felt a hovering, protective presence that soothed her soul. And her discussion with the minister had given her clearer direction by helping her focus on the essentials and clarify her thinking.

Not bad for a Sunday morning.

As she rose with a lighter heart to join Marge in the basement, she sent one final message heavenward.

Thank you, Lord, for bringing me to Oak Hill. And in the days to come, as I make some critical decisions, please help me always to ask the right questions.

Chapter Fifteen

Dale hadn't seen Christine in six days—but not for lack of trying.

He'd hoped to catch her at church Sunday, but later discovered from Marge that she'd attended the later service. Sunday afternoon he'd been tied up with a birthday party Jenna had attended. He'd stopped by the farm on Monday after he'd left the office, but Christine hadn't been home. Tuesday afternoon, he'd been committed to chaperoning a field trip for Jenna's preschool class.

At least he'd see Christine at story hour. And this week he didn't plan to sleep through the whole thing.

Since their kiss Thursday after the impromptu picnic, Dale's resolution to keep his distance had been dissolving faster than snowflakes on a hot car hood. He'd never denied his attraction to her, but he'd thought he could control it, certain the bad memories of his problems with Linda would be more than enough to keep his libido in check.

Wrong.

The last hope of that had vanished with their kiss.

Looking at Christine with as much objectivity as possible—and that wasn't much anymore, he admitted—he didn't think she bore the same debilitating scars as Linda. She was spunky and had a good sense of humor, and she wasn't afraid to share the secrets of her heart. Despite the abuse of her husband and the Dunlap sheriff, she'd held on to her self-esteem.

Yes, she still questioned her judgment. And she exercised understandable caution. There was no way she'd ever let herself be rushed into romance. But she did show a willingness to explore the attraction between them.

Now the ball was in his court.

Over the past few days, he'd thought of little but their relationship. He hadn't planned to get involved with her. Hadn't *wanted* to get involved with her. But it seemed God had other ideas. After much prayer, Dale had come to the conclusion that the Lord had sent Christine to Oak Hill for a reason that included him and Jenna.

As he and Jenna stepped through the door of the library, his gaze sought and connected with Christine's. A soft flush rose in her cheeks, and his pulse took a leap.

"Hi, Ms. Christine." Jenna pulled free of his hand and skipped over to the front desk.

"Hello, Jenna. All ready for story hour?"

"Uh-huh."

Picking up two books, she handed them to the little girl. "Why don't you take these to the story circle? They're the ones I'm going to read today. I'll be over in a minute."

"Okay."

Christine watched Jenna walk away before turning back to Dale. "You're looking much better."

"Good as new." He moved closer to the counter. "I stopped by to see you Monday afternoon, but you weren't home."

"Eleanor took a couple of days off and asked me to fill in for her."

"Including today?"

"Yes. I'll be here till four."

Disappointment rippled through Dale. He'd hoped to invite her to lunch. "How about tomorrow?"

"I'm not working again until Monday."

"Then how about joining Jenna and me for lunch?"

"Another picnic?" A smile teased her lips.

"Not this time. There's a great little restaurant in St. James I thought you might like."

She tilted her head. "Are you asking me out on a date, Sheriff?"

"Would you accept if I said yes? Because if not, I'll just say that Jenna enjoys your company, and it would be a treat for her if you came along."

"I'd like to go, but…" Yearning and uncertainty were reflected in her eyes. "I'm not sure it's wise."

"Me, neither." His reply was prompt and honest. "Ours has never been a typical relationship. But I've prayed a lot about it, and I think our meeting must be part of God's plan for us. I'm not sure we can ignore that. Or the obvious sparks between us. But that doesn't mean we have to be hasty. We both have issues to work through, and that process shouldn't be rushed."

"Slow is good," she agreed.

"Does that mean it's a date?"

"Yes."

His smile filled her with a glow as warm as the balmy late-Indian summer weather that Oak Hill was enjoying. And as she read to the children of magical castles and enchanted godmothers and happy endings, she found herself wondering if a happily-ever-after might still be in her future after all.

"There's a change of plans, Christine. I'd like to come out now, if you're available."

The smile that had lifted Christine's lips when she answered the phone and heard Dale's voice faded. There was a disquieting undercurrent in his tone she couldn't identify. He was already scheduled to take her to lunch in less than two hours. What was so pressing that he had to come early? "Sure. What's up?"

"I'll be there in fifteen minutes."

The line went dead.

She waited at the door for him, too keyed up to continue working on the talk about organic farming that Marge had convinced her to give. When his patrol car turned into her driveway, she stepped onto the porch without a jacket. The unseasonable weather was continuing, with temperatures near eighty.

Folding her arms across her chest, she watched as he pulled to a stop and slid from behind the wheel. She searched his face as he alighted from the car, looking for some clue about his abrupt call, but came up blank.

Seeing her waiting, he took the steps two at a time. Although he didn't look upset, she sensed that something was up.

He didn't keep her in suspense long.

"I heard from Andrew Briggs." As he spoke, he handed her a single sheet of paper. "This came over the fax about half an hour ago. I wanted to deliver the news in person, not by phone. Go ahead, read it."

Her heart banging against her rib cage, Christine noted the official letterhead from the prosecuting attorney's office before she scanned the document. Some of the language was legalese, but the gist was clear. Based on Gary Stratton's admission that he'd been bribed by Jack Barlow to harass Christine and fabricate charges against her, the prosecuting attorney was starting proceedings to have her record expunged. He was confident there would be no opposition to the request, and he promised to do everything in his power to expedite the process.

Closing her eyes, Christine released a slow, cleansing breath. The long nightmare was finally over. Thanks to the persistence of one man with a passion for justice. And, she suspected, a passion for her.

When she looked up at him, she had to blink to clear her vision. "You did it, Dale."

"We did it. This wouldn't have happened if you hadn't trusted me enough to tell me your story."

She shook her head. "I'd still be hiding out, hoping my past never caught up with me, if you hadn't pushed me. And believed in me. You've made the Fresh Start Farm name mean something." She held up the letter. "Do you know any more details?"

"Briggs called to alert me it was coming. The scenario played out as he hoped it would. Once he confronted Stratton with the new evidence linking him to Barlow and suggested he might have to rethink the plea bargain unless the good sheriff came clean, Stratton spilled everything." Dale touched her cheek, letting his fingers tangle in her hair. "I'd say this calls for a celebration."

"I thought you were taking me to lunch." She found herself drowning in the depths of his blue eyes.

"I am. But we have a few minutes before I have to pick up Jenna." He started to lean toward her, but paused at the sudden beep of his pager. A wry smile twisted his lips as he reached for it, his focus never wavering from her. "We'll pick this up again in a minute."

With obvious reluctance, he transferred his attention to the pager. As he read the message, his features grew taut and his lips settled into a grim line.

"What is it?"

"A possible explosive device in the basement of a high school in Rolla."

"You mean a bomb?" Her face registered shock.

"Could be."

"Why are they paging you?"

He clipped the pager back on his belt. "I spent several years on the bomb and arson squad in L.A. They like to have as many experts on hand as possible in a case like this."

"Does this happen often?" Somehow, Christine had never thought of Dale's small-town sheriff job as dangerous. Now, despite the warm day, a chill ran up her spine.

"No. And in general these calls end up being false alarms. But you can't take any chances." Twin furrows appeared on his brow. "I need to make some arrangements for Jenna."

"I can pick her up and bring her here until you get back."

"It could be late."

"I don't have anything pressing to do."

Relief flooded his face. "If you're sure you don't mind, I'd appreciate it. On days like this, I realize what a blessing it is to have Mom close by."

"I'm happy to do it. We'll bake cookies to celebrate this." She held up the letter as she followed him down the steps. "We might even save you a few."

"If you do, I'll give you a rain check on lunch. And on this." Leaning close, he brushed his lips over hers as a muted boom of thunder rumbled in the distance. He chuckled close to her ear, his breath warm against her cheek. "Interesting timing. Dramatic, but appropriate."

A gust of wind rustled the leaves at their feet, sending them skittering. Dale surveyed the horizon, where dark clouds were gathering. "Looks like we could be in for a storm."

"I wouldn't mind some rain. It would be good for the gardens." She touched his arm. "Be careful, Dale."

"Don't worry. I never take chances." With a wave, he strode toward the car.

As he drove away, Christine considered his parting remark. She had a feeling his comment was true for both his personal and professional life, especially in light of his experience with his wife. Yet he continued to see her. To let her know he cared and that he wanted to explore the attraction between them.

Watching his car disappear down the road, she said a silent prayer for his safety. And added a prayer of thanks for his willingness to take a chance on her.

"Ms. Christine, the clouds are really black now. And the wind is blowing harder."

At Jenna's tremulous comment, Christine took the

last batch of cookies out of the oven, slid them onto a rack and joined the youngster at the bay window in the living room.

She'd checked the sky herself twenty minutes ago after the wind picked up, but it had grown much more ominous in the interim. The clouds hung heavy and low, some bearing a menacing green hue. As they scuttled across the sky, shifting and swirling, they looked almost alive—and very threatening. She'd witnessed enough storms in Nebraska to know that the unusually balmy weather, coupled with a sky like this, was the perfect recipe for a tornado.

Doing her best to stifle her apprehension, Christine tried for a smile. "Why don't we listen to the radio and see what the weather people have to say while we sample our cookies?"

Back in the kitchen, Christine flipped on the light to dispel the sudden gloom. Although it was only three-thirty, the heavy clouds had masked the sun, creating twilight conditions. After she settled Jenna at the table with cookies and milk, she turned on the radio.

"…sighted in Pulaski County near Fort Leonard Wood. There have been no reports of a touchdown yet.

"Repeating, the National Weather Service has issued a tornado warning for Pulaski, Phelps, Crawford, Washington, Franklin and Jefferson Counties. A funnel cloud has been sighted in Pulaski County, and the storm is moving northeast at approximately forty miles per hour. If you live in any of the affected areas, take shelter as soon as possible. A basement offers the best protection, but an inside room…"

All at once the lights went out and the radio fell silent.

"Ms. Christine?" Jenna's wavery voice was laced with fear.

"It's okay, honey." Christine moved beside the little girl, panic gripping her. They needed to find a safe place to wait out the storm. Oak Hill was in Phelps County, between Pulaski and Crawford. They were in the direct path of the violent weather.

When Christine had purchased the house, she hadn't asked about a basement. Dark, underground places held no appeal for her. But there was a trapdoor on the outside of the house, similar to the one in *The Wizard of Oz,* that she'd never opened.

If she'd been home alone, Christine would have taken her chances and waited out the storm in an interior room. But she couldn't put the little girl at risk. She had to keep Jenna safe, no matter the cost to herself. And she needed to do it now.

Dropping down to Jenna's level, she grasped her hands. "I'm going to go outside and see if I can open the door to my storm cellar. I want you to wait here until I come back, okay?"

"C-can I go with you?"

"No, honey. It's too windy outside, and I don't want you to get hurt. I'll be back in a couple of minutes. Why don't you sing the song about the itsy-bitsy spider, and by the time you're finished I'll be back. I'll help you get started."

Doing her best to keep smiling, Christine began the simple melody. Jenna joined in, but her tone was soft and anxious. Two lines into the song, Christine rose. "You keep going. When you're done, I'll be back."

With Jenna's frightened soprano echoing in her ears, Christine grabbed a flashlight from the cabinet under the sink and headed toward the back door. As she flipped the lock and pulled it open, the force of the wind threw it back. Staggering as it slammed against her shoulder, she heard Jenna's voice falter.

Christine forced a smile to her lips as she faced the little girl, gripping the door with all her strength to hold it steady. "Keep singing, honey. I'll be right back."

She waited until Jenna picked up the melody again, then stepped onto the back porch and secured the door behind her. The wind buffeted her as she worked her way around the house toward the trapdoor, head lowered. Something blew past her face, stinging her cheek, but she ignored it. Given the way the trees were bending, she couldn't afford to waste one minute.

The rusty, long-unused hinges protested with a loud creak as she pulled up the sturdy door for the storm cellar, a task that required every bit of her strength. Flashing her light into the dark opening, Christine shuddered. The floor of the small, low-ceilinged room was dirt, and moisture clung to the stone walls. The beam of light picked up a network of cobwebs, and she heard a rustle as some small critter scampered across the floor. Surveying the small, murky space, Christine broke out in a cold sweat, her resolve to seek shelter wavering.

At a sudden ripping sound above her, she raised her head. The wind had plucked one of the heavy wood shutters off the house. The sight of it tumbling across the lawn like a matchstick galvanized her into action. Throwing back the trapdoor, she jogged toward the house, fighting down her panic. *You can do this,* she told herself. *You* have *to do this.*

Shoving her windblown hair back, she pushed through the door. The final words of the song died in Jenna's throat as Christine stepped inside, and the little girl ran to her, burying her face against the denim of Christine's jeans.

"I—I sang the w-whole song, like you said, Ms. Christine."

"I knew you would."

Extricating herself from the little girl's grip, she took the child's hand and moved around the house, retrieving the afghan from the living room and two sweaters from the closet. Throwing the items over her arm, she picked Jenna up and pressed the little girl's head against her shoulder.

"Hold tight now, okay? It's very windy outside. But it's nice and quiet and safe in the cellar. We'll sing songs and tell stories when we get there."

Without waiting for a response, Christine pushed through the kitchen door, tugging it shut behind her. Hunching over Jenna, and cupping the girl's head in a protective grip, she hurried around the side of the house.

For one brief second she faltered as she stood at the entrance to the dark cellar, fighting back her fear, trying to swallow past her nausea. *Please, God, give me the strength and the courage to do this,* she prayed.

A gust of wind pummeled her, and she staggered down the stone steps. Her blouse caught on a jagged piece of wood, but she wrenched the fabric free. Once on level ground, she set Jenna down and flipped on the flashlight. Then she went back up the steps far enough to reach the handle on the door.

Once she wrestled it shut, quiet descended. Along with suffocating darkness. The flashlight barely penetrated the gloom, and Christine began to shake.

"I don't like d-dark places, Ms. Christine."

Jenna's tremulous comment helped diffuse her own terror. Mustering every ounce of her self-control, she dropped to one knee beside the little girl. "I don't either. But this is where we'll be safest until the storm is over."

She set the flashlight on a small rock ledge in the wall and spread the afghan on the floor. After bundling Jenna in a bulky cardigan to ward off the cool dampness, she pulled the other sweater over her head. Dropping onto the afghan, she drew the little girl close, cuddling her in her arms.

"It will be okay, honey." Christine prayed that she was right. That she would be able to control her claustrophobia and keep the child safe. "The storm will be over soon, and the sun will come out again. I don't like dark little rooms, either, but it's not as scary when you have someone with you, is it? Why don't we sing another song? After that, I'll tell you some stories. Would you like that?"

She felt Jenna's nod against her shoulder, and Christine launched into a familiar melody she often sang with the children at story hour. Jenna joined in, the howling wind providing a muted backdrop to their refrain.

After the song, Christine began to tell Jenna stories. Eventually the youngster grew slack in her arms, the steady rise and fall of her chest indicating that she felt secure and safe enough to fall asleep.

If only she could do the same, Christine lamented, each agonizing second an eternity as she fought the clawing need to throw open the door and breathe fresh air.

But she couldn't give in to that temptation. Protecting Jenna had to be her priority. For the little girl's sake. And for Dale's. No matter the cost to herself.

Chapter Sixteen

"Thanks for your help, Dale." Stan Phillips held out his hand. "It's always good to have the experts on hand when something like this comes up. I'm glad it was a false alarm. Sorry we had to bother you."

The explosive device in the high school had turned out to be a knapsack filled with electrical components and wires, origin unknown.

"No problem. It doesn't pay to take chances. Never hesitate to call." Dale took Stan's hand in a firm grip. He'd worked with the Rolla police lieutenant on several occasions and respected the man's thoroughness.

As activity wound down in the basement of the evacuated school, Dale checked his watch. Four o'clock. The afternoon was gone. "If you don't need me for anything else, I'm going to head out. I have to pick up..."

"Lieutenant?"

The two men turned to the young officer who had interrupted.

"What's up?" Phillips asked.

"If you're finished here, the captain would like you to assist with the storm calls."

Parallel grooves dented the man's forehead. "Back up, Castellano. What storm?"

"Sorry, sir. I forgot you've been down here all afternoon. A storm with gale-force winds just passed through the area. No touchdowns yet, but we're getting reports of major property damage and injuries."

Fear tightened Dale's gut. "Was Oak Hill affected?"

"I don't know, sir. We're only handling calls for the Rolla area. But it would have been in the path of the storm."

"I'm out of here, Stan." Pulling out his cell phone, Dale punched in Christine's number.

"Understood. Thanks again."

As Dale strode toward the exit, taking the stairs two at a time, he listened to a message telling him there was trouble on the line. Frustrated, he slid the phone back into its holder and pushed through the door, heading for his car.

With each mile he covered on the drive back to Oak Hill, Dale's alarm escalated. Huge trees had been toppled, roofs ripped off, outbuildings leveled. And Christine and Jenna had been in the middle of it.

Flooring the car, Dale flicked on his siren. He restricted its use to dire emergencies, but this qualified.

He needed to know that the little girl he cherished and the woman he loved were safe.

The woman he loved.

Those stunning words echoed in Dale's mind as he raced toward Oak Hill. All these weeks, while he'd been agonizing over whether he could let himself care for a woman like Christine, whose problems reminded him so much of Linda's, he'd been deluding himself. A person didn't choose whether or not to care for someone. Love was stronger than that. It happened. Period.

Dale might choose not to get *involved* with Christine, but he'd had no choice about loving her. Her strength and integrity and kindness, her willingness to trust despite her fear, her humor and intelligence and sensitivity, had won his heart.

The only thing that had held him back from acknowledging his feelings had been the fear that, like his wife, Christine would be unable to move past the trauma she'd endured and open herself to love in the fullest sense, without boundaries or barriers or fears.

But she'd already proven she was capable of that, he realized. Perhaps because her trauma differed from Linda's in a very important respect. By the time Christine had crossed paths with Barlow and Stratton, her sense of identity and self-esteem were solid, thanks to the loving upbringing provided by her mother.

By contrast, in Linda's most formative years,

before she'd had a chance to develop that same re-silience and strength and grit, she'd been deprived of the unselfish love that creates stability and a solid foundation of self-worth.

In that regard, the two women were night and day, Dale concluded, finally grasping their essential difference as the miles raced by in a blur. Yes, Christine had made an error in judgment with Barlow. But a cunning manipulator could fool even the most astute person. Especially if that person had a kind heart and believed in the basic goodness of people.

And that was a perfect description of Christine.

It was why he loved her.

Yesterday, Dale had told her he thought they should take things slowly as they worked through their issues. That might still be true for her, and he would give her whatever time she needed to answer any lingering questions and put her fears to rest. But as far as he was concerned, the case was closed. He wanted to spend the rest of his life with her. And in the process, give Jenna the mother she'd always wanted.

Once Dale arrived at Fresh Start Farm, he took the driveway as fast as he dared, ignoring the frantic, metallic ping of gravel on the underbelly of the squad car. The house was intact, though two shutters and quite a few roof shingles were missing, he noted in a sweeping glance. A large white pine tree at the side of the house had also been uprooted and lay on the ground, its branches brushing the siding. If it had fallen a couple of feet to the right, it would have caused extensive damage to the house.

His pulse pounding, Dale took the front steps in a leap and pounded on the door. When an eerie silence was his only response, he moved to the rear and checked the garage. Christine's car was inside, meaning she and Jenna were somewhere on the premises.

Returning to the house, he tested the back door, stepping into a deserted kitchen when he found it unlocked. A swift perusal revealed cookies on cooling racks, a potholder on the seat of a chair and a half-empty glass of milk, suggesting a hasty departure. Papers lay strewn about the floor, as if a gust of wind had blown in through the door and sent them flying.

"Christine?"

When his voice echoed with a hollow ring and again produced no response, he did a quick inspection of the house. Hoping to find a set of steps leading to a basement, he tried all of the doors on the first floor, but they all led to closets.

Planting his fists on his hips, Dale tried to rein in his rising panic. They had to be here somewhere. Christine was too smart to take refuge in an outbuilding. That would be the first to go in a tornado. A basement was the safest place.

Given that the farmhouse was old, might there be an exterior entrance to a cellar? he wondered. Moving back outside, he circled the structure, looking for a trapdoor. And found it, half-hidden by the branches of the downed white pine.

With a silent prayer that he'd find them inside, safe and secure, he grasped the heavy wooden door and pulled, the rusty hinges announcing his arrival with a loud creak.

The sight that met his eyes sent relief coursing through his veins even as it twisted his gut.

Christine was sitting on the dirt floor, her back against the wall, a sleeping Jenna nestled in her arms. His daughter was wrapped in two bulky sweaters, her lashes sweeping across her rosy cheeks, and she looked fine.

But Christine didn't. Her face was white, and there was a long, bloody scratch on one cheek. One sleeve of her cotton shirt had been almost ripped off at the shoulder, and her hair was in disarray. Even from a distance he could see that she was shivering as she blinked in the sudden light.

Descending the stone steps, Dale went down on one knee beside her, touching her cheek, her hair, her arm, needing to reassure himself that she was okay.

"Is it over?" Her words came out in a hoarse croak as she tried to focus her glazed eyes.

"Yes." He lifted Jenna into his arms. "Wait here. I'll be back in a minute."

His daughter roused a bit as he hurried toward the house, looking up at him sleepily. "Hi, Daddy. We had a storm."

"I know."

"Where's Ms. Christine?"

"In the cellar. I'm going to go back and get her as soon as I take you into the house."

She yawned. "We sang songs and Ms. Christine told me stories until I fell asleep. But I didn't like it down there. It was too dark. And I was cold until Ms. Christine gave me her sweater. She didn't like it down there, either."

Knowing the severity of Christine's claustrophobia, that had to be the understatement of the year, Dale concluded, his jaw tightening. Left alone, he doubted she'd have considered going into that dark hole, preferring to take her chances with the storm. But she'd put aside her own fears to keep Jenna safe, enduring yet another reminder of the trauma Barlow had subjected her to.

The love he already felt for her swelled, contracting his heart with a tenderness so intense it was almost like a physical ache.

After settling Jenna at the table with a cookie, he sprinted back around the house, half expecting to find that Christine had emerged. But she remained where he'd left her, her back propped against the wall, her eyes wide and dazed in her colorless face.

He descended the steps, ducking under the low ceiling to crouch beside her. "Let's get you out of here." His voice was gentle, his touch strong and sure as he gathered her into his arms.

With his help, she managed to stand, and he followed her up the narrow steps, one hand supporting her at her waist. The storm had left cooler weather in its wake, and when a chilly breeze blew past, her shivering intensified. Putting an arm around her, he urged her toward the house.

"Let's get inside where it's warm."

The electricity hadn't yet been restored, and night was falling fast. After pulling out a chair and urging her into it, Dale scrounged up some candles from a kitchen drawer, fitted them into some makeshift holders and set them on the table. Then he retrieved a heavy sweater from the hall closet.

The candles didn't provide a lot of light, but enough to confirm his initial assessment of her condition. The experience had taken both an emotional and physical toll. She looked shell-shocked and injured. He'd already noted the long, angry scratch on her cheek. But as he bent to drape the sweater around her, a purple bruise on her shoulder peeked out through the jagged tear in her shirt.

Bending close, he eased the fabric aside to get a better view. The contusion was four inches across, and she flinched as he touched it.

"The back door slammed against me when I opened it to g-go out. It's just a b-bruise."

He wasn't convinced of that, but he gently draped the sweater around her shoulders and focused on the cut on her face. "You have a nasty scratch on your cheek."

"It's bleeding," Jenna offered. "Does it hurt?"

"Not too much, honey." Somehow Christine managed the semblance of a smile.

Dale rose. "Where are your first aid supplies?"

"In the bathroom. Bring aspirin, too."

He didn't need to ask why. The strain around her eyes and the lines at the corners of her mouth were clear indications she was battling a major headache.

Once back in the kitchen, he filled a glass with water and handed her four aspirin. She swallowed them all at once.

"Let's have a look at that cheek." As he pulled up a chair beside her, she angled her head to give him access to the scratch. He did his best to be gentle as he cleaned the cut and treated it with antiseptic ointment, but she tensed a few times, and a single tear trailed down her cheek. "Sorry, Christine. I'm trying not to hurt you."

"I know. It's okay. I appreciate your help."

Up until now, Jenna had watched Dale's ministrations in interested silence, elbow on the table, chin propped in hand. But she, too, noticed the tear. "Are you going to cry, Ms. Christine?"

At the little girl's troubled expression, Christine dredged up another smile. "No. It just stings a little bit. I'll be fine in a minute."

"I cut my chin last summer when I fell off my bike. That hurt, too, and I cried a lot. I had to get stitches from Dr. Sam."

"Well, that's much worse than this. I don't even need stitches."

Finished, Dale gathered up the supplies and stowed them back in the first aid kit. He still didn't like Christine's color, and she continued to shiver despite the heavy sweater.

"I'm not crazy about the idea of leaving you alone tonight." He considered his options, settling on the one that would cause her the least stress. She'd already had more than enough of that for one day. "Why don't Jenna and I stay? Between the window seat and couch, we'll be fine."

"No." Gratitude tightened her throat, but she shook her head. "Take Jenna home. She's had a tough day."

"So have you."

"I'll be fine. I'm going straight to bed as soon as you leave and I'll probably sleep till morning. Is the house okay?"

"No major damage that I could see. A couple of shutters are gone, and a few roof shingles were ripped off. You lost the pine tree, too, but it missed the house. I can take a closer look tomorrow in the daylight, after I pick Mom up at the airport." He leaned close and touched her face. "You're sure you'll be okay alone?"

Looking into his warm, caring eyes, Christine didn't feel alone. And she had a strong intuition she never would again.

"You'll be close if I need you."

In response to her tender smile, the blue of his irises deepened in color. "Count on it."

They left a few minutes later, Jenna's hand tucked into Dale's. Christine went to bed at once, as she'd said she would. But as she drifted to sleep, Dale's final comment echoed in her mind.

He's said that she could count on him. That he'd be close if she needed him.

And she didn't think he'd been referring only to tonight.

For the past week, Christine had been reflecting on the questions Reverend Andrews had posed for her consideration. All at once the answers seemed clear.

No, she didn't want to let fear win and live the rest of her life alone. Yes, she did believe that Dale was who he appeared to be. And yes, she was willing to put her trust in the Lord and open her heart to love. Because she had come to believe that God meant for them to be together. For always.

It might take Dale longer to arrive at that conclusion, Christine reminded herself. He had heavy baggage to deal with, too. But she was filled with a serene confidence that the Lord would reveal it to him, in time, as He'd done for her.

All she had to do was wait.

And keep reminding herself of that inspiring passage from Corinthians that spoke to the power of love.

So there abide faith, hope and love, these three;
but the greatest of these is love.

Leaning on her hoe, Christine surveyed her
pumpkin patch. With Stephen's help, she'd spent the
morning cleaning up her storm-ravaged herb and
flower gardens and listening to the high-schooler
rhapsodize about his girlfriend.

Though his help had been forced on her in the beginning, she now looked forward to his visits. He
worked hard and seemed to enjoy learning about
organic farming. In fact, he'd expressed an interest
in a paying job once he worked off his penalty for
the reckless driving incident.

She could have used his help this afternoon, too,
considering the mess in the pumpkin patch, Christine
reflected. But at least her sound sleep had left her
feeling as fresh and energized as the sunny, crisp
autumn day that had followed on the heels of the storm.

Thankfully, neither the farm nor her body had
suffered any permanent damage from the gale. Others
hadn't been so lucky, as she'd learned from the
morning news. Property damage had been consid-
erable, and dozens of people had sustained injuries.

As she set to work, Christine replayed in her mind
the phone conversation she'd had with Dale that
morning before he and Jenna left to pick up his
mother at the airport. They hadn't spoken long, but
he'd promised to stop by as soon as he got back. As

a result, when she heard the sound of a slowing car half an hour later, her pulse accelerated.

Shading her eyes, she watched as he set the brake and stepped out of the car. In many ways, the scene reminded her of his first visit. He'd been in uniform that day versus his attire today of jeans and a black leather jacket, but her reaction was the same. Her heart skidded to a stop and the breath jammed in her throat.

On this occasion, however, her response had nothing to do with fear.

A slow smile lit his face as he walked toward her, and the warmth in his eyes reached deep inside her. She half expected him to greet her with a kiss, but to her surprise he stopped several feet away and shoved his hands into his pockets.

"Hi." His husky, intimate tone about did her in, and she leaned on the shovel to prop up legs that suddenly didn't feel too reliable.

"Hi. Is your mom back safe and sound?"

"Yes. And she's already been drafted into babysitting duty. I had some important business to attend to, and I didn't want Jenna tagging along."

"Business?" She gave him a quizzical look.

"Of a personal nature."

He took one step closer, then another, erasing the distance between them. Leaning down, he fitted his lips to hers, lingering, tasting, and at last releasing—with reluctance.

"You'll notice I kept my hands in my pockets." His

voice wasn't quite even, and he drew an unsteady breath. "That's because I'm fighting a very strong urge to pull you into my arms and never let go. But I have a few things to say first."

Jamming his hands deeper into his pockets, Dale gave her a rueful smile. "I suppose there are better ways to do this. More romantic settings. But the storm was a wake-up call. As I raced back to Oak Hill yesterday, terrified at what I might find, I was reminded that there are no guarantees about tomorrow. And I didn't want to wait one more second to let you know how I feel.

"From the day we met, I sensed there was something different about you. And as I got to know you, I realized my instincts were correct. You were not only different, but very special. I was impressed by your strength, and touched by your kindness and consideration. I admired your integrity, enjoyed your sense of humor and respected your efforts to reconnect with the Lord. And being a man, I couldn't fail to appreciate your beauty." His lips quirked into a quick grin.

"What I'm trying to say, Christine, is that I fell in love with you. I didn't want to, not after all the problems I had with Linda. But it happened. And I've come to realize that the two of you aren't as similar as I first thought. You haven't let your problems control your life. You've done your best to leave them behind, and while caution prevents you from trusting or confiding in haste, it doesn't cripple you. You're willing to trust when the trust has been earned, and to open your heart. Linda could never do that."

Tugging the hoe from her grip, he set it aside and took her hands in his. "You also care about Jenna. And what you did yesterday for her, despite your claustrophobia…" His voice choked, and his Adam's apple bobbed as he struggled for control. "You have a great capacity for unselfish love, Christine. More than any person I've ever met. And you deserve the same in return."

He cupped her face with his hands, and the love shining in his eyes dazzled her more than the brilliant autumn sun. "I've thought about this and prayed about it, and I know we were meant to be together. But I understand that you need time. I just want you to know how I feel, and that I'm willing to wait."

He nodded toward the pumpkin patch and a smile whispered at his lips. "I'm afraid I can't turn pumpkins into coaches, or wave a magic wand and make life perfect. But if you'll marry me, I can promise you I'll do my best to love you and cherish you and make every day of the rest of your life better than the one before."

As she stared into Dale's eyes, blue as the sky above them and filled with profound, abiding love, Christine was too overcome with emotion to speak. Instead, she wrapped her arms around him and held on tight, letting his solid presence reassure her that he wouldn't evaporate like Cinderella's coach and leave her once more alone in her pumpkin patch.

When the silence lengthened, Dale pressed his lips to her hair and stroked her back. "I didn't mean to rush you, Christine. I'm sorry if…"

"No." She cut him off and sucked in a deep breath, backing up far enough to see his face. "You haven't. I just…I never expected…I love you, too." And rising on tiptoe, she pressed her lips to his, putting all the emotion she'd been unable to express in words into that kiss.

For a moment Dale seemed taken aback by her ardor. But he recovered quickly and pulled her close, giving her an enticing hint of the depth of his own feelings.

Drawing apart at last, Christine was content to rest in the circle of his arms as she looked up at him. "Wow."

He grinned. "Can I interpret that as an acceptance of my proposal?"

"I think that would be a safe bet." She smiled. "How does a spring wedding sound to you?"

"That's five months away."

"I thought you said you were willing to wait?"

"That was before that last kiss." He grinned, letting his fingers play with the silky strands of her hair.

"I wouldn't mind a longer courtship this time."

At her sudden note of uncertainty, his levity vanished and his fingers stilled. "I was only teasing, Christine. I'd wait five years for you, if that's what it took. And spring would be appropriate. It's the season of new beginnings and fresh starts. Just like the sign says." He inclined his head toward the entrance to her property.

Gazing at the placard she'd erected when she first came to Oak Hill, her expression grew pensive. "You know, when I named this place, I never expected the fresh start to include love. And a family." A tender smile lifted her lips in a gentle curve. "Maybe there's something magical about pumpkin patches, after all."

"Maybe." He pulled her close again, and as he looked down into the soft brown eyes he'd come to love, he gave thanks. For magic. And miracles. And most of all, for a second chance at love.

When Dale lowered his lips to hers to seal their engagement, Christine, too, sent a silent thank-you heavenward. She might never understand why the Lord had given her such a difficult road to follow. But she would be forever grateful that it had led her into the arms of this special man, who had taught her how to trust and to love again.

As she surrendered to Dale's embrace, joy filled Christine's heart. Once upon a time, she'd believed in Prince Charming. Then life had convinced her that he lived only in the pages of fairy tales.

But she'd been wrong. Prince Charming had come to her very own pumpkin patch. And in his arms, she knew she would live happily ever after.

* * * * *

Dear Reader,

With *Where Love Abides,* we say goodbye to Oak Hill, Missouri, where three couples found hope—and love—deep in America's heartland. In this last book in my HEARTLAND HOMECOMING series, Christine is able to wipe clean the slate of her past with the help of a very special man…and give the name of her property, Fresh Start Farm, new meaning.

Starting over is never easy. It takes courage and strength and perseverance to tackle the unknown. But when we put our trust in the Lord and open our hearts to love, the journey can be a joyful one that offers unexpected rewards. And, as Christine discovers, it can also lead to a happy ending.

To learn more about my next book—and all my latest news—I invite you to visit my Web site at www.irenehannon.com.

May all your journeys be joyful, and may all your endings be happy.

Irene Hannon

DISCUSSION QUESTIONS

1. In *Where Love Abides,* Christine's negative experience with a sheriff colors her perceptions of Dale. Can you think of instances in your own life where you judged a person based on experiences that have nothing to do with him or her? How did your preconceived ideas affect that relationship? How *should* we approach new people? Why?

2. As a single dad, Dale must juggle the demands of parenthood with those of his job. How well do you think he handles this balancing act? Cite some specific examples of behavior from the book that support your opinion.

3. When the book begins, Christine doesn't want to owe anyone anything, fearing that debt can be used to manipulate her. Have you ever experienced a situation where someone tried to use emotional blackmail to manipulate you? How did you deal with it? How did your faith help you address it?

4. Christine married after a whirlwind, fairy-tale courtship. What are the dangers of rushing into marriage? What are the advantages of a longer courtship?

5. Dale is committed to justice and to righting wrongs. What does the Bible tell us about these principles? Why is it often hard to live by them, especially in today's world?

6. What qualities in Dale begin to soften Christine's attitude toward him? What fears hold her back from giving him her trust—and her heart?

7. Christine is estranged from the Lord when the book begins. She feels as if He abandoned her, that her prayers went unheard and unanswered. Yet Reverend Andrews tells her that God never turns away from us, even when we turn away from Him. Why is this hard to accept for many people? What are some ways a person might try to re-establish a connection to the Lord when they feel lost or abandoned?

8. Dale's first wife never overcame her issues with childhood abuse, leaving him wary of damaged women. But in the end, he realizes that Christine's positive self-image, formed in childhood, has allowed her to overcome her trauma. What does this say about the importance of giving a child a loving, stable upbringing?

9. Reverend Andrews tells Christine that accepting without understanding is one of the great chal-

lenges of faith. Do you think this is true? If so, give some examples from your own life that left you puzzled about God's ways, and discuss how you made peace with them.

10. Erin stayed in an abusive relationship because she felt she had no recourse—until Christine offered her the gift of friendship and helped her see that she had other options. Have you ever felt trapped in an intolerable situation? How did you deal with it? How did the support of friends or family help you address the situation? What role did your faith play?

11. At the end of the book, Christine finds the strength to face her claustrophobia in order to keep Jenna safe. Her selfless act calls to mind the passage from Corinthians, "Love bears with all things, believes all things, hopes all things, endures all things. Love never fails." Talk about the power of love—and how it has been manifested in your life. What are some things love has prompted you to do that you otherwise wouldn't have done?

Love Inspired®

HEARTWARMING INSPIRATIONAL ROMANCE

Contemporary,
inspirational romances
with Christian characters
facing the challenges
of life and love
in today's world.

**NOW AVAILABLE IN REGULAR
AND LARGER-PRINT FORMATS.**

Steeple
Hill®

For exciting stories that reflect traditional values,
visit:
www.SteepleHill.com

Love Inspired®
SUSPENSE
RIVETING INSPIRATIONAL ROMANCE

Watch for our new series of
edge-of-your-seat suspense novels.
These contemporary tales
of intrigue and romance
feature Christian characters
facing challenges to their faith...
and their lives!

**Steeple
Hill®**

Visit:
www.SteepleHill.com

HISTORICAL

INSPIRATIONAL HISTORICAL ROMANCE

Engaging stories of romance,
adventure and faith,
these novels are set in
various historical periods
from biblical times
to World War II.

NOW AVAILABLE!

Steeple
Hill®

For exciting stories that reflect traditional values,
visit:

www.SteepleHill.com